JACK STRONG
TAKES A
STAND

TOMMY GREENWALD

JACK STRONG TAKES A STAND

Illustrations by
MELISSA MENDES

ROARING
BROOK
PRESS

NEW
YORK

SQUARE
FISH

SQUARE FISH

An Imprint of Macmillan
175 Fifth Avenue
New York, NY 10010
mackids.com

Square Fish books may be purchased for business or promotional use.
For information on bulk purchases, please contact the Macmillan
Corporate and Premium Sales Department at (800) 221-7945 x5442
or by e-mail at specialmarkets@macmillan.com.

Library of Congress Cataloging-in-Publication Data

Greenwald, Tom.
Jack Strong takes a stand / Tommy Greenwald ; illustrated by Melissa
Mendes.
pages cm
Summary: Tired of being forced to participate in sports and take extra
lessons and tutoring to become well-rounded in anticipation of college, middle-
schooler Jack Strong stages a sit-in on his couch until his parents ease up.
ISBN 978-1-250-05687-0 (paperback) / ISBN 978-1-59643-838-5 (e-book)
[1. Family life—Fiction. 2. Strikes and lockouts—Fiction. 3. Middle
schools—Fiction. 4. Schools—Fiction. 5. Humorous stories.] I. Title.
PZ7.G8523Jac 2013
[Fic]—dc23

2013001325

Originally published in the United States by Roaring Brook Press
First Square Fish Edition: 2015
Book designed by Andrew Arnold
Square Fish logo designed by Filomena Tuosto

1 3 5 7 9 10 8 6 4 2

AR: 4.5 / LEXILE: 640L

To Michele Rubin and Nancy Mercado,
for obvious reasons

And to parents and children everywhere,
who try to find the right balance every day

JACK'S SCHEDULE

DATE	6	7	8
DAY	MONDAY	TUESDAY	WEDNESDAY
TIME	7:30 SCHOOL	7:30 SCHOOL	7:30 SCHOOL
TIME	4:00 SOCCER	4:00 TENNIS	4:00 SWIMMING
TIME	6:00 DINNER	5:30 TEST PREP TUTOR	5:30 MATH TUTOR
TIME	7:00 HOMEWORK	6:30 DINNER	7:30 DINNER
TIME	8:30 CELLO PRACTICE	7:00 HOMEWORK	8:00 HOMEWORK
TIME	9:30 BED	8:30 CHINESE HOMEWORK	9:30 CELLO PRACTICE
		9:00 CELLO PRACTICE	10:00 BED
		9:30 BED	

9	10	11	
THURSDAY	FRIDAY	SATURDAY	SUNDAY
7:30 SCHOOL	7:30 SCHOOL	9:00 YOUTH ORCHESTRA	10:00 CELLO LESSON
4:00 FREE TIME	4:00 KARATE	12:00 CHINESE CLASS	12:00 JUNIOR EMTS
6:30 DINNER	5:30 LITTLE LEAGUE PRACTICE (LEAVE EARLY)	1:30 LITTLE LEAGUE PRACTICE	2:00 LITTLE LEAGUE CHAMPIONSHIP GAME
7:30 HOMEWORK	6:45 DINNER	4:00 FREE TIME	5:00 TENNIS
9:00 CELLO PRACTICE	7:30 CELLO RECITAL	7:00 DINNER	7:00 DINNER
9:45 BED	10:00 BED	8:00 FREE TIME	8:00 HOMEWORK
		10:00 BED	9:30 BED

JACK STRONG
TAKES A
STAND

PART 1
BEFORE

1

I was about to go to soccer practice when I decided to go on strike.

I didn't mean for it to become this big thing.

I was just feeling kind of tired, that's all.

But the next thing I knew, there were two big television trucks outside my house.

There was a stage on my front lawn, with lights mounted on twenty-foot poles. There was a television host sitting right next to me. There was an audience gathered in front of the stage, full of people. Half of them thought I was a hero, the other half thought I was a menace to society.

And they were all there because of *me*.

Just because I sat down on a couch.

Who would've thought?!

But first, a little background information.

My name is Jack Strong, but I used to wish it wasn't.

I know, it sounds like a cool name. And it *would* be a cool name, if I actually *were* strong. But I'm not. Just lifting my ridiculously heavy backpack in the morning is a challenge.

The truth is, I'm kind of weak.

Which the other kids think is hilarious, of course.

I go to Horace Henchell Middle School. It's a typical middle school. The classrooms are way too hot, and the cheeseburgers are way too cold. No one knows who Horace Henchell is, but it's generally assumed that he is both well respected and dead.

I do really well at the school part of school. My grades are excellent, and the teachers like me. I don't make trouble.

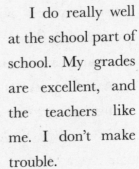

The non-school part is a little harder for me. I'm not what you would call a loser or anything, but I'm definitely not at the top of the heap, either. I'm in that huge middle section of kids who mind their own business and try to get through the day without any real drama. Usually it works. I'm not a great athlete, and I don't think the modeling agencies will be calling anytime soon, but some people seem to think I'm pretty funny. Every once in a while I make a joke in class that the other kids laugh at, and that's enough to keep me off the list of dorks and lame-os, at least for the time being.

I have one really good friend, Leo Landis, who I've eaten lunch with every day since second grade, and one really bad enemy, Alex Mutchnik, who's hated me ever since he was caught cheating off my math quiz last year. (I didn't tell on him, but he hates me anyway.) Alex's favorite activities are knocking my backpack off my shoulders and gluing my locker shut.

You know, typical school stuff.

But I definitely don't hate school. There's a lot about it that I like.

For instance, there's Cathy Billows, who's so pretty that it makes my eyebrows hurt. There's Mrs. Bender, my favorite teacher, whose tiny but unmistakable mustache makes me smile every time I see it.

And there's the bus ride home.

The ride home is incredibly important because it's the one time of day I have completely to myself. I always sit in the same seat: third row back, window seat on the left. The seat next to me is usually empty, but I don't mind—it gives me a place to put my backpack. And as the bus slowly rolls away, I gradually begin to put the school day behind me.

"Have a nice night, Horace," I say. And then—using my jacket as a pillow—I rest my head against the window, smile, close my eyes, and think about my absolute favorite thing in the world.

The couch.

To someone who doesn't know any better, our couch is no great shakes.

It has one or two rips in it, from when my dog, Maddie, makes herself comfortable a little too aggressively. It has plenty of stains—soda stains, sauce stains, chocolate stains, and several mystery stains. And it might not surprise you to learn that it smells a little, too. My mom always talks about getting rid of it, but I won't let her.

Because to me, that couch represents everything good.

It's where I watch *Dancing with the Chimps*, my favorite TV show. It's where I play *Silver Warriors of Doom II*, the video game that Leo and I would happily play until we are old men, if only our parents would let us. It's where Maddie lies down on my lap, even though she's way too big to be a lap dog.

It's where I daydream about Cathy Billows.

It's where I forget about Alex Mutchnik.

It's where I eat a huge bowl of Super Fun Flakies every day after school.

I could go on and on, but I think you get the picture. The couch is pretty much my favorite place in the world.

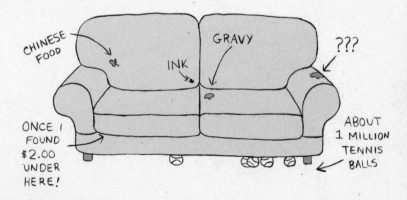

CHINESE FOOD

GRAVY

???

INK

ONCE I FOUND $2.00 UNDER HERE!

ABOUT 1 MILLION TENNIS BALLS

The only problem was the outside world kept inter-rupting.

Because here's the thing: I was probably the most overscheduled kid in the entire universe. Or, at least, I was tied with all the other overscheduled kids. And there wasn't anything I could do about it.

And then came the week of June 6.

2

It all started after school on Wednesday, June 8. I was just settling in on the couch.

"JACK!"

I prepared myself for the second blast, which was definitely coming.

Wait for it . . .

"JACK!"

There it was.

My mom ran into the room.

"Have you seen my phone?"

My mom is the world's absolute greatest person, but she has two problems: she can never find her glasses and she can never find her phone. Sometimes, the fact that she can't find her glasses means that she can't see well enough to find her phone.

"No, Mom, sorry. I haven't."

She sighed. "Well, what else is new? Dad is going to kill me." The one thing my dad can't stand is when he tries to call my mom and she doesn't answer. Which happens probably around, oh, let's say sixty-two times a day.

Mom slapped my leg. "What did I say about leaving your shoes on in the house?"

"What's the point of taking them off?" I complained. "I just have to put them back on in ten minutes anyway."

"Still." That was my mom's answer for everything, when she didn't have an actual answer.

My grandmother, whom I call Nana, came into the room from the kitchen. Nana is seventy-four years old, but she has more energy than anyone in the family. She's my mom's mom, but my dad thinks of her as his mom, too, since his parents died a pretty long time ago.

Nana was eating a tongue sandwich, as usual. She loved tongue, which may be the grossest meat ever invented by man. I think it's from a cow. She made me try it once. It was so salty my mouth dried up on the spot. It's also bad for you. It's especially bad for people with heart problems, like Nana, but she didn't care.

"How can you eat that?" I asked, which was the same question I asked every time.

NANA'S
TONGUE
SANDWICH:

RYE BREAD
TONGUE!
HORSERADISH
DILL PICKLES
MUSTARD

"You don't know what you're missing," she said, which was her usual answer. "Want to watch my story with me?" A "story" is one of the daytime reruns she loves, usually old crime shows like *Law & Order* or *Magnum, P.I.* or something like that. She's also a TV news and politics junkie, I think mainly because she loves talking about how wrong most people are and how the country is falling apart.

"I can't, Nana. I have to go to swimming."

Nana shook her head. "Swimming schwimming." She looked at my mom. "Why do you make this boy run all over town doing silly things? Can't he just sit and relax with his grandmother? Is that so wrong?"

My mom shrugged as if she'd had this conversation a thousand times, which she had. "It's important to stay active," she said. "It helps kids stay focused."

"Says who?" asked Nana. "You or Richard?"

Richard is my dad.

"I don't have time to talk about this right now," grumbled my mom. Then she glared at me, as though it were my fault she had a mother. "Go get your bathing suit."

Nana waved her arms in disgust as she took a seat on the couch. It was an ongoing argument in our house. My dad wanted me to be in afterschool activities pretty much every waking hour. He said it would make me well rounded and help me figure out what I was most good at—"my thing," he likes to call it. Then, once I discovered what "my thing" was, I could focus on it and get great at it before applying to college.

That was the plan, anyway.

My mom didn't care nearly as much as my dad did about that kind of stuff, but she trusted him, and usually went along with what he wanted.

Meanwhile, Nana and I thought the whole thing was a little crazy. I don't even like swimming. I mean, swimming in a pool at a friend's house on a hot summer day is one thing, but going to the Y after a long school day is not my idea of a good time. But my parents thought it was important for me to become a good swimmer. Just like they thought it was important that I study Chinese, play soccer, learn the cello, volunteer at Junior EMTs, and have a math tutor.

And that was just during the week. On the weekends, you could throw in Little League and youth orchestra.

I think maybe it's because I'm an only child that my parents pay so much attention to me, and shower me with love, and help me find a gazillion ways to improve myself. Or maybe it's because practically every parent in America is obsessed with making sure their kids are experts at every activity ever created by humans.

Whatever the reason, I was busy twenty-four hours a day, seven days a week. And even though I didn't like it, I accepted it. Just like most kids accept it. Because we're too lazy not to.

Anyway, I got my bathing suit and off we went. I turned the car radio up, and my mom immediately turned it down.

"How was school today?"

"Alex Mutchnik decided it would be funny to tape my hair to the desk."

My mom smacked the steering wheel. "I'm going to call his mother!"

"No, you're not."

She looked at me, which was a little scary, considering she was also driving the car at the time. She did that a lot. "That kid sounds like such a nightmare."

"He is a nightmare, but he's my nightmare, so let me deal with it. Your job is to watch the road, so you can drive to the Y without killing me."

My phone buzzed. I didn't recognize the number. Who would be calling me? The only person who ever really called me was Leo.

"Hello?"

"Hi, Jack? It's Cathy!"

My heart did a weird little somersault. Cathy Billows. The prettiest girl in the entire state, last I checked. Calling *me*! My first thought was that she needed help on a homework assignment or something.

I tried to play it cool. "H-hey, Cathy. Wh-wh-what's going on?" Playing it cool is hard, it turns out.

"Not much!" Cathy is one of those girls who always talks in exclamation points. "How about you?"

"I'm on my way to swim class."

"Oh, awesome!" Not really, which we both knew. "Well anyway, Jack, I just wanted you to know that I'm having a party Friday night to celebrate the end of the school year, and I thought you might want to come!"

"Me?"

"Yup!" Cathy giggled. "Everyone in homeroom is invited, so we can tell stories about the whole year! You can tell a funny story or something, since you're kind of funny. It'll be great! Please come—it will be so much more fun if the whole class is there!"

"Oh, wow, that does sound like fun." I think I must have turned some strange color right about then, because my mom looked at me—still driving, of course.

"Who is it?" she whispered, way too loudly.

"Watch the road," I whispered back, turning toward the window.

I spoke quietly into the phone. "Well, um, I have to ask my parents, but yeah, I'd totally love to come."

"Awesome! Bye!" And just like that, she was gone. A potentially life-changing conversation, over in less than a minute.

I put the phone in my pocket and prayed that my mom wouldn't start firing questions.

"Who was that? What did they want?"

My prayers went unanswered.

"Nobody, and nothing." We were almost there. I found myself actually looking forward to getting out of the car and going to swimming.

"Oh come on, tell me," badgered my mom. "It sounded like a girl."

"I don't want to talk about it right now, okay?" The truth was I didn't want to talk about it *ever*. Because I already knew there was a problem with Cathy's invitation, and I was pretty sure there wasn't a solution.

My mom sighed. "Okay." She could be annoying sometimes, but when it came right down to it, she respected my privacy. She's pretty cool that way, I guess.

When we got to the Y, I hopped out of the car before my mom could think of any more questions.

"See you in an hour," I said, sprinting up the steps.

I could barely hear her say, "Okay, honey. I love you," before the door closed behind me.

3

I don't need to bore you with the details of my swimming class. All you need to know is that we concentrated on the backstroke, which happens to be my least favorite stroke. I'm not sure how mastering the backstroke is going to help me get into a good college. You'll have to ask my dad that one.

And I definitely don't need to bore you by talking about the session I had with my math tutor after swimming. Technically, I suppose it could help with the college math test I'll need to take in high school. Unless I forget everything, which, considering the test is about five years away, is entirely possible.

So let's get right to the unboring part.

The night started out pretty much like every other night. My dad came home at his usual time, meaning after my mom and I had finished dinner. (Dad has a job in "overseas markets." I have no idea what that means except for the fact that he works a lot. So does my mom, even though she doesn't have a *job* job.)

Dad sat down to dinner, and Nana joined him.

"When are you going to admit that the president is doing a lousy job?" Dad asked her.

"As soon as you admit your guy would have been ten times worse," Nana answered.

Then they proceeded to argue about politics the entire meal, the way they do every night. They love every second of it.

After dinner, my mom and my dad sat down on the couch to watch TV while rubbing each other's feet. That was also a nightly ritual—and it was the only time I ever saw them completely relax. Nana thought it was adorable. I thought it was kind of gross.

I decided to make my move halfway through their TV show, when they would be at their peak of relaxation.

"Mom? Dad? I have a question."

My dad put the show on pause.

"What's up?" asked my mom.

"Well, I got a call today from Cathy Billows, who's like this really popular girl in our school."

"I hate that word," said my mom, meaning *popular*. She was the type of person who wanted all kids to be popular.

My dad looked curious. I didn't get a call from a popular girl every day. Or any girl, for that matter.

"What did she want?"

"Well, that's the thing," I said, shuffling my feet. I was nervous, probably because I knew what was coming. "She invited me to her party Friday night. It's kind of a big deal. I really want to go."

My dad leaned back on the couch with a big sigh. "Well, that's bad timing. You have your cello recital Friday night, which obviously you can't miss."

I felt my whole body get stiff. "Why not? Why can't I skip the recital, just this once?"

"You can't skip the recital," my dad said. "I don't care if the president himself invited you to the White House. You made the commitment to the cello, and this recital is the most important event of the year."

I flopped down on a chair. "I didn't make the commitment to the cello, you did!"

My mom looked at my dad. "Honey, maybe just this once—"

"Not just this once," my dad said, the volume of his voice starting to increase just a bit. "He goes to the recital, and that's it!"

Maddie hated fighting, so she gave a worried little bark and left the room. Nana, on the other hand, never missed a fight, so she came in.

"I can't believe this," I said. "This is ridiculous. I never get to do anything I want to do!"

"He's right," said Nana. "Let the kid live a little, for God's sake."

"Rose, you're not helping," my dad said, calling Nana by her real first name.

"Well, I'm not hurting," said Nana.

My mom tried to hug me, but I squirmed away. "Honey, there will be other parties," she said, "but this recital is very important, and you're such a wonderful cellist."

She was right. I was pretty good. And I actually liked playing the cello, usually. Right then, I couldn't stand it.

"But, hey, that's great you got invited," said my dad. "And the fact that you can't go will just make them want you even more next time."

"What next time?" I said. "Who says there's going

to be a next time? I don't know what it was like when you went to middle school, but kids like me don't usually get a second chance. Thanks for nothing."

And with that, I went upstairs to not do my homework.

4

"Whatever," Leo said, shrugging his shoulders.

"What do you mean, whatever?"

It was the next day at lunch, and I was telling him about the party invitation, the cello recital, and the fact that my dad had ruined my life.

Leo shook his head, his long curly hair flying all over the place. "So you miss the party. I don't get what the big deal is."

"What the big deal is? This is Cathy Billows we're talking about here! SHE called ME. On the PHONE. And she called me 'FUNNY'!" (Actually, she'd said "kind of funny," but Leo didn't need to know that.)

I sat back in my chair and took a sip of chocolate milk, reliving the memory of the phone call for approximately the 4,385th time.

"Sometimes I wish music had never been invented," I whined.

"Music is important," said a voice from the next

table. I turned and was shocked to see it was Lucy Fleck. She was an amazing piano player who went to the same music school I did. I'd never heard her say a word outside of class before.

"Um, okay," I said.

"More important than Cathy Billows's party," Lucy added.

"Uh-oh. Speak of the devil," Leo mumbled. I looked up and saw Cathy's bright green eyes, jet-black hair, and flawless bone structure.

"Hi, Jack!"

"Hey," I tried to say.

Alex Mutchnik was standing right behind her, which was completely unsurprising, since he had a thing for her. Alex nodded at me, but not in a good way.

Cathy smiled, and I could swear one of her teeth actually sparkled. "So, I just wanted to make sure you were coming to my party tomorrow night!"

"Did you have to invite the *whole* homeroom?" Alex butted in.

I decided to stand up and take my punishment like a man. "Well, here's the thing," I began. "I would love to go, I completely and totally would, but as it turns out I have this major cello recital, and my parents won't let me skip it."

Alex reacted first by sneering, "Your *parents*?"

Cathy was frozen. It was like she couldn't process the fact that someone would turn down an invitation to one of her parties. Finally, she blinked once.

"A cello recital?" she asked, as if I'd said it in Swahili.

I nodded. "Yup. I know, it's a bummer."

"A bummer for YOU," offered Alex.

"Why don't you stay out of it," Leo said to Alex bravely.

"Why don't YOU stay out of it," Alex responded uncreatively.

Meanwhile, Cathy was beginning to process the fact that I would not be attending her party. Her smile faded and was replaced by a stare that was so cold it's probably illegal in several countries.

"Fine."

No exclamation point this time.

Then she shook her head and walked away without another word.

Alex had one word left, though.

"Loser."

5

The cello recital, like all recitals, had a strict no-escape policy. Which basically meant, if there were twenty-eight musicians performing and your kid was third, you didn't get to sneak out the side door after he or she performed.

I think they might have even locked everyone inside.

I was twenty-third on the program, so by the time I went, most of the audience was tired and resentful. People were staring out the window. Cell phones were burning holes in pockets. And there was a lot of coughing and shuffling.

I began to play one of Bach's unaccompanied sonatas. And here's the funny thing: even though I was so mad at my parents—and mad at my cello, mad at basically everything and everyone—when I started to play, I forgot all about it. I got into the music. Like I said, I really like the cello. And I sounded pretty darn good.

Until I looked up and saw Mrs. Fleck.

Mrs. Fleck is Lucy Fleck's mother. I told you Lucy was quiet, and an amazing piano player. But I didn't tell you that she has the craziest mother in America.

Mrs. Fleck is the most intense person I've ever met, by far. She makes my dad seem like a marshmallow. She goes everywhere her daughter goes, watches her do everything, screams the loudest at her soccer games, claps the loudest at her concerts, complains the loudest when her grades are less than straight A pluses.

And not only that—she's one of those parents who doesn't like it when other kids do well.

So when I was playing my cello and I happened to look up and see Mrs. Fleck, she was staring at me and making this face that basically said, *I hope you drop your bow.*

So what did I do? I dropped my bow.

Yup. I did. It slid right out of my hand and clattered across the wood floor. Everyone gasped. Even the parents who had fallen asleep were suddenly wide-awake.

I sat in my seat for a second, not sure what to do. Then I mumbled "sorry," went and got my bow, sat back down, and finished the piece. But the magic was gone.

I hated the cello again.

Afterward I went back to my seat, my ears burning with embarrassment. Two people later, Lucy Fleck performed some incredibly hard Beethoven piece on the piano and was amazing. She actually got a standing ovation. Mrs. Fleck jumped up and down like a kangaroo on steroids.

Meanwhile, all I could think about was that somewhere across town, Cathy Billows was having a party that I'd been invited to. Alex Mutchnik was there, probably telling dumb stories that everyone was laughing at, because I wasn't there to tell funny ones.

What was wrong with this picture?

Everything.

6

After the recital, there were snacks and juice in the lobby. Kind of like a reward to the audience for making it all the way through.

"I thought you were fantastic," said Nana, chomping on a cookie.

"Thanks, Nana."

She could tell I was upset, so she tried to cheer me up by smacking me on the head, which was kind of an unusual method. "What the matter? So you dropped the bow? I'm sure Casals dropped his bow all the time!" Pablo Casals was like the most famous cellist of all time, and I'm pretty sure he never dropped his bow in his entire life.

"I guess so," I mumbled, more than ready to change the subject.

My mom and dad were a couple of feet away, talking to some other parents about how wonderful we all were. Eventually they made their way over to me.

My mom hugged me. "Fantastic, honey!"

My dad was smiling, but I could tell he was thinking about the bow incident. "Great job, Jack."

"Sorry about the bow," I said.

He shook his head. "Hey, it happens. You didn't let it get to you; you plowed right through it. That takes guts. I'm proud of you."

Then he hugged me, too. I felt like I had disappointed him, and I was mad at myself for caring that I disappointed him, but I hugged him back.

"Let's get ice cream," Nana announced, and I immediately felt better. Ice cream is a much better way to cheer up a grandson than a smack on the head, by the way.

On our way out we passed Lucy Fleck, surrounded by her family. Mrs. Fleck was taking pictures and shouting at her daughter, trying unsuccessfully to get her to smile. Lucy saw me and came over.

"I'm sorry you dropped your bow," she said.

"Thanks. You were awesome tonight."

"Thank you." Lucy still didn't smile. I'm not sure she knew how to smile. Maybe because Mrs. Fleck was her mother.

"LUCY, WE NEED YOU! EVERYONE WANTS

A PICTURE OF THE STAR PIANIST!" shouted Mrs. Fleck.

"I have to go," Lucy said to me, and went back to her mom.

Nana shook her head at Mrs. Fleck. "Something is wrong with that woman," she announced, way too loudly.

My mom went white. "Mom, sshhh!"

My dad chuckled.

"What?" said Nana. "She's a whack job, and I don't care who knows it."

Luckily, the whack job was too caught up in her daughter's amazingness to hear a word my grandmother said.

7

"How was the party?"

It was later that night, and I was on the phone with Leo, who wasn't actually at the party, but who had talked to David Cussler, who was.

"David said it was pretty fun, until Alex pushed Becky into the pool with her clothes on, and her cell phone was trashed," Leo reported. "Then Becky started to cry, and when her brother came to pick her up and found out what happened, he smacked Alex on the back with his lacrosse stick, and Alex got so mad he left the party and just started walking down the street and never came back. Apparently his dad ended up picking him up at the Stop & Shop on Westlake."

I whistled. Wow, there was a lot of action at these parties. And I was no fan of Alex Mutchnik's, but walking all the way to Stop & Shop by yourself on a dark night sounded pretty scary.

"How was your cello recital?" asked Leo.

"Horrible," I answered, without going into details.

"That's too bad. What are you doing tomorrow? Do you want to meet downtown or something?"

I sighed. "I don't know. I have orchestra at nine, Chinese at noon, and baseball practice at one-thirty."

"Dang," Leo said, "I thought I had it bad."

After I got off the phone, I lay down on my bed

and tried to make myself think that it was good I didn't go to the party after all. I imagined spilling a drink on some fancy rug, and then knocking over a lamp while trying to clean it up.

But then I imagined Cathy Billows trying to cheer me up and help me forget about my clumsiness by dancing with me and holding my hand.

Ugh. The last thing I wanted in my imagination right then was a happy ending.

8

There were twelve kids in my Chinese class, and half of them were Chinese-American. I guess their parents wanted them to speak the language of their ancestors. I already spoke the language of my ancestors, at least going back to my great-grandparents. My great-great-grandparents were from Europe somewhere, but according to my dad, Chinese is a more important language to learn than French or German, or even Spanish.

"It's the future," my dad said. "Did you know the United States owes more than a trillion dollars to the Chinese? If you know the language, you'll be able to write your own ticket in this world. Yup, China is where's it at."

Yeah, well, China may be where it's at, but Chinese class was where I was at on a beautiful Saturday afternoon, and I wasn't too happy about it. Neither was anyone else. Even the Chinese kids.

Oh, and did I mention that Chinese has its own alphabet? As if learning a foreign language isn't hard enough.

"Okay class, let's review last week's lesson," said our teacher, Ms. Li. She was okay I guess, but very strict. I was obsessed with her glasses. She wore them so close to the tip of her nose that I kept staring at them, waiting for them to fall. But they never did.

I opened up my book and stared down at the page. We were in the middle of a unit about items in the house.

"Lamp," said Ms. Li.

"*Deng*," we all chanted.

"Table."

"*Ji.*"

"Brush."

"*Hao.*"

"Window."

"*Chuang.*"

BUZZZZ!!!

No, *buzzzz* is not a household item. It's the sound a phone makes when a text is coming in.

More specifically, it's the sound MY phone makes when a text is coming in.

BUZZZZ!

I froze, a little shocked that I actually forgot to turn off my phone. If there's one thing Ms. Li can't stand, it's phones going off in the middle of her class.

Everyone turned around to stare at me.

The teacher's eyes narrowed. "Well, Mr. Strong, are you going to tell us all what's so important?"

"You mean, you want me to see what it says?"

"Please."

I fumbled for my phone and opened the text. It was from Leo. I read it quickly, swore a little under my breath, and then put the phone back in my pocket.

"Well?" asked Ms. Li.

I hesitated. This wasn't really a text I wanted to share with the class.

"Well?" she repeated.

"Um, it said that today is Sundae Saturday down at Super Scooper. Free sundaes from twelve to one."

Evelyn Chang, who never says a word, actually giggled a little bit.

Ms. Li nodded. "I see. Well, that's very nice to know—"

BUZZZZ!

Omg. Again?

"I'm so sorry," I mumbled.

Ms. Li walked over, stood right over me, and stuck out her hand. Her glasses dangled dangerously close to the cliff of her nose. I took the phone out of my pocket and handed it to her. She opened it.

"'THE WHOLE TOWN IS HERE,'" she read out loud. "'WHY CAN'T YOU SKIP CHINESE JUST THIS ONCE AND COME DOWN?'"

This time *everyone* giggled.

Does the word *blush* come from combining the words *blood* and *rush*? Because that's what happened to my face. I got incredibly red, I think my nose started to run, and little drops of sweat started popping out all over my body.

It wasn't fun.

Ms. Li handed me back my phone. "You might want to turn that off."

My mind was a jumble of Chinese lamps and hot-fudge sundaes. First the cello recital fiasco, and now this. Here I was again, stuck someplace I didn't want to be while everyone else in the world was hanging out and having fun, like normal human beings.

I turned off the phone and put it in my pocket.

Ms. Li smiled.

"By the way, the Chinese word for ice cream sundae is *sheng dai.*"

雪糕

9

After my mom picked me up, I asked her to take me down to Super Scooper. Even though the Sundae Saturday special offer was over, maybe I'd run into a few kids, and I'd get a milkshake out of the deal.

My mom thought for a second. "Don't you have baseball practice? It's important that you go, right? Big game tomorrow?"

"Practice is at one-thirty. I'll be fine. Come on, mom." I was trying to be nice, since I really wanted that shake, but I was running out of patience.

"Okay, you deserve it," she said, sensing my mood. Moms are good at that. My mom is, at least.

But by the time we got downtown, there was only one person there.

Cathy Billows.

She was sitting outside polishing off her free sundae, licking the spoon clean. I don't think I'd ever seen her alone before, and it didn't look natural. Maybe she was waiting for a ride. In any event, one thing I did know is that I didn't want her to see me. I was trying to figure out how to avoid her when she spotted me.

"Hello, Jack." No exclamation point, but at least no stare of death, either.

"Hey. So, I'm really sorry I couldn't make your party last night. I heard it was awesome."

She almost smiled at the compliment. "It was pretty awesome. At least, until Alex started acting like a jerk."

It was my turn to smile. Finally, the rest of the world was discovering what I'd known for years: that Alex Mutchnik was the world's most annoying person.

"Yo, Strong!"

I turned around. Cathy's brother Baxter was running toward us, grinning from ear to ear. Baxter Billows was a grade above us, and he was the happiest person I'd ever met. Probably because he was really good-looking, really good at sports, and really popular. I'd be happy all the time, too, if I were even one of those things.

Baxter stopped and caught his breath. "Traffic is horrible," he said to his sister, "so Mom wanted me to tell you to meet her at the post office." Then he turned

to me. "We got practice in an hour. You gonna be ready? Big game tomorrow!"

I tried to sound confident. "Yeah, I'm definitely going to be ready."

By some fluke of nature and birthday cut-offs, Baxter and I wound up on the same Little League team, and the championship game was the next day. Since he was the star and I was, well, let's just say *not* the star, we had different definitions of "being ready." His definition was taking an hour of batting practice and two hours of fielding practice. My definition was being able to find my hat.

Baxter smacked me on the back, which kind of hurt a little. "All right dude, see you at the field." And off he went.

"Well, I better get going, too," said Cathy. "See you later."

"Bye, Cathy!" I said. Great. Now I was the one using the exclamation points.

My mom, who was sitting in the car, leaned out the window. "Was that Baxter? He's such a nice kid."

There was no higher compliment in the world than being called "nice" by my mom, by the way.

"Yeah, he's really nice."

I headed inside to get my consolation prize milkshake. Ricky, the kid who worked there, was reading a magazine.

"Hey, bro," he said.

"Hey, Ricky. If my milkshake isn't the best milkshake ever, I'm going to call your boss."

"That'd be just fine with me."

Ricky and I always joked around like that. Working

there seemed like it would be an awesome job, so I always pretended I was going to get him fired and take his job, and he always pretended that I could have it.

"How's school going?" I asked him. Ricky was already in college.

He shook his head. "Not going this semester. I'm just gonna take it easy and work for a while."

Wow. Working in an ice cream store *and* taking it easy?

Some guys have all the luck.

10

At practice I managed to hit the ball out of the infield twice. Which was three fewer times than Baxter Billows hit the ball over the fence.

"How'd it go?" asked my dad when he picked me up.

"Really good."

About three traffic lights later, I said, "But, Dad? I don't really think I'm cut out for baseball. I think this will probably be my last year playing."

My dad turned the radio down, which he did whenever he was stressed in the car. And he would get stressed in the car for two reasons: a bad traffic jam and a stubborn son.

"I thought you just said it went really well."

"Yeah, by my standards. Which means that I didn't trip over my own feet running around the bases. By those standards, today's practice was a total success."

"Jack, listen to me," my dad said. "I can't tell you

how important it is to be well rounded. It's not enough to just be smart these days. You need to play an instrument, be involved in the community, do some volunteer work, and play a sport."

"Why can't I just do karate? Karate's a sport."

My dad shook his head. "Karate is an exercise that helps your coordination and stamina for the real sports, like soccer and baseball. Plus, you actually *like* baseball."

That was true. I did actually like baseball. As long as I was watching it on TV and not playing it.

"Maybe it's team sports you're not crazy about," my dad suggested. "What if I sign you up for some tennis lessons? Tennis is a great game."

I just wanted to end the conversation. "Whatever."

"Whatever yourself," my dad said. "All I'm saying is, colleges look at all that stuff."

"Don't you think it's a little early for me to be worrying about college? I have all of high school to deal with that."

"It's NEVER too early to be thinking about college and finding that thing that will set you apart. Do you have any idea how competitive it's gotten out there?"

I was starting to get mad. "Actually, no, I don't. Why would I? I'm in MIDDLE SCHOOL."

My dad turned the radio completely off. "Listen, Jack, I know you think I'm a crazy lunatic. Sometimes I think I am, too. But I'm the one out there in the world, not you. I'm the one who sees how hard it is to get ahead and how hard people have to work. I know you're a kid. I get it, I swear. But if you don't learn the value of hard work now, I'm afraid you're going to fall behind. And these days, once you fall behind, it's incredibly hard to catch up."

"You're right about one thing," I said. "You ARE a crazy lunatic."

I turned the radio back on, way louder than before, and neither one of us said another word until we pulled into the driveway. But as I was getting out of the car, I turned to my dad and said, "I'm twelve years old. I would appreciate it if you didn't bring up college ever again until I'm sixteen. I just want you to let me live my life and do the things I want to do and be a kid. I don't see what's so bad about that."

Then I smacked the hood of the car with my hand before I went inside.

It was the hardest hit I had all day.

11

Sunday, before the big game, I had a cello lesson and junior EMTs.

I bet Derek Jeter never warmed up that way.

Anyway, the cello lesson was fine, because I love my teacher, Dr. Jonas, and since he's a big baseball fan, he took it easy on me. "After the season is over, though, I'm going to work you to the bone," he said.

Then I had to go to Junior EMTs, which was a volunteer organization where kids learned emergency medical procedures. My dad made me join because he was an EMT when he was younger, and I guess he helped save some guy's life in college. And also, because supposedly it looked good on a college application, which I guess makes sense if you're applying to college. I wasn't. I wasn't even ready to apply to high school.

"Don't worry about that part of it," my mom would say. "Just think of it as a way to help people."

She had a point, of course. The only problem was—and I hate to admit this—helping other people wasn't that high on my list. Especially on a Sunday morning between a cello lesson and the baseball championship game.

The EMT class was at the fire department. "Tell mom to pick me up fifteen minutes early," I said to Nana, who was dropping me off on her way to play golf. "I need to get to the field for early batting practice."

"Isn't it a little late to practice?" said Nana, who wasn't a very big baseball fan. "The game's in two hours. Shouldn't you know batting by now?"

"You would think," I told her.

I walked into the firehouse, where there were four dummies—by "dummies" I mean fake bodies, not dumb people—laid out on the floor. We were learning how to do CPR, which basically means trying to get someone breathing again by pressing on their chest and blowing air into their mouths. There were only four of us in the class—me and three high school kids who totally ignored me—so we got a lot of individual attention from the teacher, Lieutenant Sniffen. This was not a good thing.

I was busy pressing on my dummy's chest, and trying to get up the courage to put my mouth on it, when Lieutenant Sniffen came over to inspect my technique.

"You're doing it too gently," he said. "Our job is to save the person, not tickle them."

I shrugged. "Sorry."

"And what kind of resuscitation technique is that?" he asked. "It's called 'mouth-to-mouth' for a reason."

The other kids laughed.

"Hey!" barked Lieutenant Sniffen. "Saving lives is not a laughing matter."

He leaned down right over me. "If you were having a heart attack, would you want me to be the last person you see?"

I looked up at his face, which had a big brown mole on the left cheek.

"Not really."

"I didn't think so." Then he brought his mouth so close to my mouth, I could feel the hairs of his mustache. "And would you want these lips to be the last lips you kissed?"

"Definitely not."

"I didn't think so," he said. "But if I didn't do my job right, my ugly mug and my hairy lips would be your last memory for all eternity."

Finally he backed up. "Now get back over there and push and blow like you mean it."

With Lieutenant Sniffen watching my every move, I went back over to my dummy, pressed hard on its chest, and then somehow managed to put my mouth on its mouth. It tasted like wet socks. I blew. I saw the dummy's chest rise and fall.

"By George I think you've got it!" roared the Lieutenant. "Good work, son!"

I think he was waiting for me to thank him, but I was too busy gagging.

When my mom came to pick me up, I still had the gross wet-sock taste in my mouth.

"How was it?" she asked.

"Completely disgusting," I answered.

"Well, I'm very proud of you, Jack. You never know when all this training is going to come in handy."

I got in the backseat. "I do know. It's going to come

in handy when I apply to some fancy college and I can say I saved a dummy's life. Whoop-de-doo."

Then I changed into my baseball uniform to get ready for the big game.

Where I could be the dummy.

12

I'm not really sure why they call the Little League championship game in my town the "World Series," unless you think the entire world consists of approximately sixteen thousand people.

But that's what they called it: the World Series, and it's surprising how many people go to watch this game. Even people who have no immediate family connection to anyone involved. Which is just kind of weird, if you ask me.

Anyway, my team—the Pirates—was playing the Astros. Baxter Billows was our pitcher, and he was mowing them down, like usual. But so was Kevin Kessler, the pitcher for the Astros. See, the thing about Little League is that on every team, there are always four or five kids who are way better than everyone else, and they're always pitchers, and they always strike out everyone who bats sixth in the order and below. That's just the way the world works. But these two guys, Baxter and Kevin, they were so good they were striking *everyone* out.

After about forty-five minutes, we were already into the fifth inning, because nothing was happening except for strikeouts. The score was 0–0, and I was due up next inning for my one and only at-bat (everyone had to bat at least once). I glanced over to the bleachers where I saw Cathy Billows playing with a dog. *My* dog. Maddie was wagging her tail, and Cathy was laughing. Sometimes I wished *I* were a dog.

Then I saw my parents sitting one row over. My mom was talking with somebody—I would say she watched about one pitch per game, the rest of the time she was yakking—and my dad was fiddling with the video camera, getting ready for my big plate appearance. In front of them sat Nana, who was wearing a big hat and reading the *New York Times*. It was adorable, how she still read the actual newspaper. Who does that?

It was still 0–0 in the bottom of the sixth. I was due up fourth. The good thing was that Kevin Kessler had pitched an inning in his last game—and a kid can only pitch six innings a week—so they had to bring in a new pitcher.

Who turned out to be Alex Mutchnik.

As he took his warm-up pitches, he looked over at me and grinned. "You're up this inning?"

I ignored him, so he tried again. "I am so scared."

"Shut up, Alex," I said.

"That's enough out of both of you," barked the first base umpire, a scary old guy appropriately named Mr. Barker.

We were toward the bottom of the order, where the lame kids bat, so nobody was expecting much. Sure enough, the first kid, Sherman Wexler, struck out on three pitches. The second kid, Pete Coluski, struck out on four pitches. But then Jeffrey Siffriani, who was famous for not having swung at a single pitch during the entire season, walked on a full count. The dugout stirred. The bleachers took notice. Even Nana looked up from her newspaper. Everyone seemed to realize that if I could somehow get on base, our lead-off hitter—the one and only Baxter Billows—would have a chance to win the game.

I stepped up to the plate. Alex stared in at me and fired. The pitch was wild, but I swung at it anyway. Ugh. But the good news was that the ball got by the catcher, so Jeffrey was able to go to second.

"Come on, Jack!" I heard my dad holler from behind his camera. "Only the good ones! Only the good ones!" Thanks, Dad. Easy for you to say.

The second pitch was about a foot over my head, and I almost swung at it, but I managed to stop myself. Alex was getting wild, I thought to myself. Maybe if I just hang on I can work out a walk like Jeffrey did. How great would that be? To not make the third out would be so awesome—

The next pitch was right down the middle and the bat didn't budge from my shoulder.

One ball, two strikes. Oh, great. Strikeout, here we come. So typical.

But then the next two pitches were balls. Full count. I began to hope for a walk again.

Alex wound up and threw. The pitch came, a little high, quite possibly ball four, but for some crazy reason I decided to swing anyway. I probably closed my eyes, because according to Dad's pictures I always close my eyes when I swing. So I never saw the bat hit the ball.

PING!!

The sound of the aluminum bat hitting the ball may have been the most awesome sound I'd ever heard in my life.

I opened my eyes. At first I couldn't locate the ball, but suddenly there it was, on a high arc, soaring, flying, a towering shot heading right for . . . the second baseman.

Okay, so it wasn't exactly a monster home run.

But here's a little secret I'll let you in on. A lot of little leaguers can't catch a high pop. Especially during the last inning of a World Series game, when everyone is screaming "RUN!" and "GO!" and "OH MY GOD!!!"

So poor little Michael Bostwick dropped the ball. Well, to be technical about it, it dropped about two feet behind him.

After that, everything seemed to happen in slow motion. I stood on first base and watched relatively chunky Jeffrey Siffriani motor around third and chug for home. It took Michael Bostwick a couple of seconds to retrieve the ball, and that was all the time Jeffrey needed. He slid . . . the ball came in . . . a cloud of dust . . .

"SAFE!" hollered the umpire, a pimply tenth grader named Clay McLeod, who probably just wanted to go home.

Game over. We won the World Series, 1–0. And I was the hero, thanks to my pop-up to second base.

All of a sudden I was totally mobbed. A chant went up: "Jack! Jack! Jack!" Alex Mutchnik angrily threw his glove on the ground. Baxter Billows lifted me up and gave me a hug that may have broken several ribs. Cathy Billows was jumping up and down. My mom was jumping up and down. Nana was jumping up and down. Maddie was under the bleachers, scavenging for scraps. And my dad was filming it all.

As I stood there, soaking it all in, I thought to myself: I could get used to this whole hero thing.

13

After the trophy presentation and the free cake, it was finally time to pack up our stuff and leave the field. On our way to the parking lot, Cathy came running over to me.

"Jack! That was amazing!" The exclamation points were back.

"Thanks. I just got lucky, but thanks."

"So listen," Cathy said, twirling her hair with her finger "we're going over to the Dirty Dog to celebrate! Baxter said it'd be fun if you wanted to come!"

OMG. The Dirty Dog had the best hot dogs and root beer floats in the entire state. And Cathy was welcoming me back into her inner circle. This was too good to be true!

But my dad was already shaking his head.

"Well, this is lousy timing. I just signed you up for that tennis clinic that starts today."

You have GOT to be kidding me.

"What tennis clinic?"

My dad sighed. "We just talked about this yester-day! You agreed to start trying out some individual sports, so we thought we'd give tennis a try?"

Was he kidding? Since when is saying "whatever" a sign of agreement?

Nana interrupted. "Oh come on, Richard, let the boy have some fun. He just hit the game-winning home run, for God's sake."

"It was a pop-up," I corrected, "but thanks, Nana."

My mom tried to compromise, as usual. "Can we just go to the Dirty Dog for a little while before tennis?"

My dad glanced at his watch. "Hmm. These les-sons are pretty pricey, and every minute counts. Why don't we just go celebrate after the clinic?"

That was it. That was the moment I realized my dad would never, ever get it. I threw my glove on the ground.

"THE POINT IS NOT TO CELEBRATE AFTER THE CLINIC! THE POINT IS TO CEL-EBRATE WITH MY *TEAMMATES*! THE POINT IS TO HAVE FUN LIKE A *NORMAL* KID!"

Wow. I wasn't sure where that came from. I'd never really lost it like that before.

It felt good.

"And I don't like tennis," I added softly.

No one said a word. Everyone in the whole parking lot was staring at me, waiting to see what I'd do next. *I* was waiting to see what I'd do next.

But it turned out I wasn't quite brave enough to take a stand against my father.

(Yet.)

So after a minute, I picked up my glove and walked over to the Billows's car.

"I can't go, but thanks anyway."

"No problem," said Cathy, who looked at me as if I were a different, more dangerous person.

Baxter smacked my arm. "Great hit, dude."

"Thanks."

I walked back over and got in our car. I didn't look at anyone.

The only one who dared to speak was Nana.

"I don't like tennis, either," she said. "I prefer golf."

14

The day after my baseball triumph-turned-disaster, I found myself Leo-less at lunch (he was out sick) and looking for a place to sit. The only open spot was next to Lucy Fleck.

"Can I sit here?" I asked.

Lucy was staring at some weird healthy food thing that her crazy mom probably made her eat. "Yes."

We ate in silence for a few minutes. Then suddenly she said, "Congratulations on your game-winning hit yesterday."

I nearly dropped my fish stick. "You heard about that?"

"Yes. Everyone's talking about it."

"Well, cool, thanks. It wasn't really a hit, though. I got kind of lucky."

She managed to look at me a little. "You made contact in a crucial situation. You put the ball in play, which is the main thing. After that, the burden falls to the team in the field, and as we all know, anything can happen in Little League. You did your job. Well done."

I looked at her, thinking: Who IS this person?

She took a deep breath. I think she was exhausted by her speech.

"So, do you play any sports?" I asked.

"I fence."

That figured. Fencing was like squash, one of those completely weird sports that a lot of parents were starting to make their kids do, because no one else was doing it. Which, when you think about it, doesn't exactly make sense.

"Do you like it?"

She put her fork down and looked directly at me

for the first time. "Of course I do. It helps me learn dexterity and discipline. I also figure skate in the winter."

"Cool," I said. "Well, if you're as good at sports as you are on the piano, you must be awesome."

"Thank you," Lucy said. "I have to go."

I watched Lucy put her tray away and walk out of the cafeteria. She didn't seem to mind being overscheduled. Why couldn't I be more like her?

Because I couldn't, that's why.

15

Then came Monday afternoon, June 13.

When I got home, I threw my backpack down by the front door, got myself a giant bowl of cereal, grabbed the remote, and dove onto the couch.

It was more comfy than usual.

Maddie joined me about five seconds later and started fighting me for the cereal. I won, as usual, but she got her fair share.

I turned on the TV. So much was on. I finally narrowed it down to two of my favorites: *Pencilneck*, a cartoon about a kid who was half human and half pencil, and *Now What?!?*, a reality show where four really good-looking teenagers have to live without their smartphones for a week.

I couldn't decide, so I flipped between the two for about twenty minutes. Then I fell asleep. It was awesome!

Then it wasn't awesome.

I felt a tap on my toe. Then the tap got a little harder. Then someone was shaking my whole foot. Then I was awake.

"Jack? Jack? Come on honey, time to go."

I opened my eyes unwillingly.

"Go where?"

My mom and Nana were looking down at me, and mom was holding my soccer cleats. I guess that was my answer.

"We don't want to be late."

I looked at her. "YOU don't want to be late. I want to be extremely late." I closed my eyes again.

"Jack, seriously."

I sat up and rubbed my eyes. "Mom, I'm really tired. Really, REALLY tired. Can't I skip soccer just this once? We don't even have to tell Dad."

"I think that's a fine idea," said Nana. "Jack and I will sit here and watch a little television. It's too rainy for soccer anyway."

"It's barely drizzling," said my mom, but she kind of looked like she didn't have the heart to fight about it. For a minute, I allowed myself to think that I might actually get to spend an entire afternoon just hanging out on the couch!

Then my mom's cell phone rang.

As usual, she couldn't find it. While she was running around looking for it, it rang two more times.

Looking back on it, it's funny to think that if my mom hadn't found her phone, this whole crazy thing might not have happened.

But she found it.

"It's Dad," she said.

Nana and I sighed.

"Hi, honey," my mom chirped into the phone. She had a really cheerful phone manner. "What's up?" She listened for a second, then glanced at me. "We're about to," she said into the phone. "He's tired." Another beat, then she said, "He doesn't." Nana and I watched as Mom nodded at something my dad said, then added, "It was a very busy weekend, Richard, busier than

68

usual!" After two more seconds of nodding, she held the phone out to me. "He wants to talk to you."

"Poor kiddo," Nana said, shaking her head.

I took the phone as though it were a plate of asparagus. "Hey, Dad."

"Mom tells me you don't want to go to soccer?" As usual, not a lot of intro chitchat from Dad.

"I'm really tired, and I just want to watch a little TV with Nana today."

My dad's sigh into the phone sounded like a hurricane. "I get that, Jack, I really do. And you can watch a little TV tonight before homework, I promise. But right now you have to go to soccer. Remember, while you're sitting around, all the other kids are out there, getting better."

It was my turn to sigh. "Dad, do you really want to know what the other kids are doing? I'll tell you. They're at the party you didn't let me go to because I had to get better at the cello. And they're getting the free ice cream sundaes that I missed because I had to get better at Chinese. And they're celebrating winning the World Series, but they're celebrating without me, because I had to get better at tennis. So don't tell me about the other kids."

"And *you* don't talk to me that way," my dad said, in his *watch it* voice. "I let you scream in the parking lot after the baseball game because I knew you were feeling upset that you couldn't go celebrate with the team, and I got that. But that's enough. I mean it."

Whenever Dad talked to me like that, I usually responded by not responding. But this time—maybe because I was tired, or maybe because I was fed up, or maybe because of the expression on Cathy Billows's face when I yelled at the baseball field—I did respond.

"Whatever, Dad. I'm not going to soccer practice today, and that's final."

Out of the corner of my eye, I saw my mom shaking her head, and my nana smiling just a tiny bit.

My dad was silent for minute. I think he was trying to decide whether he was going to blow up at me or try to play it cool.

"So what you're saying," he finally said, playing it cool, "is that you'd rather be one of those kids who just sits on the couch all day long, watching TV, playing video games, doing nothing? Is that what you're telling me?"

I didn't answer.

My dad asked again. "Is it?"

I stared at the phone, thinking about his question. Then I thought about all the times Leo and I would be just starting a video game when I got interrupted because I had to go, and I thought about telling Cathy I couldn't go to her party, and about Lucy Fleck's crazy mother making me drop my bow, and about Lucy

Fleck herself, who seemed like she didn't really know how to smile, and I thought about all the things I did every day that I didn't really want to do, and most of all I thought about lying on the couch, relaxing. Just relaxing. It sounded so simple, and yet I'd never really done it. Because even when I was just hanging out, I always had one ear out, listening for the footsteps, the jingle of the car keys, the loud voice I knew was coming, which meant it was time to go to some other activity I really didn't want to go to.

And then I had a sudden flashback to last summer, when my friend Charlie Joe Jackson took a stand at Camp Rituhbukkee when they wanted to add an extra class, and how brave and awesome that was. Why couldn't *I* do something like that?

I looked at Nana. She nodded her head once. "It's totally up to you," she said.

And I realized she was right. It WAS totally up to me.

Suddenly I knew what I was going to do. What I HAD to do.

"You know what, Dad?" I said into the phone. "I think I do want to become one of those kids who just sits on the couch all day long. And you know what else? I want to become one of those kids who sits on the couch all night long, too! In fact, I want to become one of those kids who sits on the couch all the time! How's that sound?"

My dad didn't say anything, but I could hear him breathing.

"And I'm not getting off the couch ever again, for anything," I announced, surprising even myself. "EVER," I repeated, in case he hadn't quite heard me. "Or at least until you let me quit all the stuff I don't like doing."

I stopped, held my breath, and waited for my dad to say something. It took about eight seconds.

"Put Mom on the phone," he said.

I handed the phone to my mom, who immediately went into the other room and started whispering like crazy.

Nana looked down at me.

"Really?" she asked.

"Really," I answered.

She shook her head and smiled, as I flipped on the TV and settled in.

It was official.

I was on strike.

PART 2

DURING

16

STRIKE—DAY 1

It took a while for my parents to realize I was serious.

I spent the rest of that first day on the couch, hanging out with Nana, reading, and watching *Columbo*. When Dad got home, Maddie got off the couch to greet him. I didn't.

He didn't bring up our earlier conversation. All he said was, "Whatcha watching?"

"A bunch of stuff," I answered.

"Great," said Dad, heading back into the kitchen for dinner. Nana joined him, as usual. But my parents didn't come in to watch TV and rub each other's feet, which was unusual.

About an hour later, Nana came back in. "I'm heading to bed," she announced, looking at me. "Are you coming?"

"Nope."

She smiled. "What are you up to, Jack Strong?"

I looked up at her. "I don't know exactly. But I'm staying here."

I expected her to tell me I was being silly. Instead, she said, "Let me get you a blanket."

After another half hour, my parents came in.

"Are you planning on sleeping here tonight?" my mom asked.

"Yup."

"You're a stubborn one," said my dad, rubbing my head.

"Wonder where he gets that from," my mom said, laughing.

"We'll talk about this tomorrow," my dad said, not laughing.

Mom kissed my cheek. "Sleep well, honey."

I did.

17

STRIKE—DAY 2

The next morning, I was still on the couch when my mom came in to wake me up for school.

"I'm not going."

My mom looked around for help, but there was none. Nana was still asleep, and Dad was long gone. He usually left for work at like 5:45.

It was just the two of us, unless you count Maddie, who had wandered in to see what was going on.

"What do you mean, you're not going?"

I rolled over and dug my head into the pillow. "I mean, I'm not going to school."

"Are you sick?"

"Sure."

"Let me get a thermometer." As she left the room, I sat up and considered my options: Stop the madness and get up and go to school, stall and pretend to be sick, or take a stand.

I looked at Maddie, who was wagging her tail. She looked like she was ready for a little excitement in her life. And you know something? So was I.

When my mom came back with the thermometer, I said, "Actually, I'm not sick, Mom. I'm just not going to school."

"And why not?" she asked, even though I think she knew the answer.

"Because I'm not getting up from the couch. Like I told you guys last night, I'm not getting up until you guys let me quit some of my stupid activities."

"I'm going to call your father."

"Fine. Go ahead."

The lack of fear at the mention of my dad's name made her stop in her tracks. She came back and sat down next to me on the couch. "What is up with you?"

"Nothing." I sat up next to her. "It's just that you always want Dad to do the dirty work, to be the bad guy and yell at me, or something. Well, he can't make me change my mind this time, and neither can you. I'm staying on the couch. I'll have Leo bring my homework, and I'll keep up with my schoolwork, but I'm staying here. And that's final."

I waited to see what my mom would do. It was true that she was way too nice to ever get really angry at me, so she left all the unpleasant stuff to my dad (and then of course she got mad at him if he yelled at me too loudly). But this time I thought she might actually get mad at *me*, since I called her out on it.

Instead, she just sighed heavily, realizing she wasn't going to change my mind.

"Well, I guess it's okay, just for today. But what about when you're hungry? How are you going to get food? And what about when you have to go to the bathroom?"

"I've already decided—there are some things I can get off the couch for," I said. "Like, to get food from the kitchen, and to go to the bathroom, and to charge my phone. And Nana and I talked about doing some exercises to the TV, while standing next to the couch, but that's it. Otherwise, I'm staying right here." And I patted the cushion.

My mom smiled a little. "You've really thought this through, haven't you?" I think she might even have been a little proud of me, in a way. "Okay, fine," she added. "I'll call the school. But we need to get all this figured out tonight when Dad gets home."

Maddie somehow sensed that the situation was resolved—at least for now—and she jumped up onto the couch next to me.

"I know one family member who's happy with your decision, anyway," my mom said, petting Maddie.

"Two," said Nana, plopping down on the other side.

18

What a great day!

First, Nana and I exercised in the morning. (Yoga is incredibly hard, by the way.) Then I watched some TV, checked out some YouTube, played some video games, listened to music, read a little bit, took a nap, played with Maddie, had a delicious lunch, and went to absolutely no organized activities of any kind.

After lunch, my mom and Nana went shopping, so I had the house to myself for two hours. It was awesome.

Around dinnertime, I got a text from Leo: WHERE WERE YOU TODAY??

I texted back: LONG STORY. CALL ME.

Six seconds later, the phone rang.

"Dude, what's up? Are you sick?"

"Nope," I answered, playing it cool. "Not sick."

"Then what? Why weren't you in school today?"

I took a deep breath. "Because I'm staying on the couch and not getting up."

"You're what?"

"I told my parents I'm not getting up from the couch until they agree to let me give up some of the stuff I'm always signed up for, like karate and Chinese and stuff like that."

"Holy moly," Leo said, getting right to the point as usual. "So you're on strike? Like that Polish guy?"

I'd told Leo awhile back about Charlie Joe Jackson, and how he'd been inspired to lead a mini-strike at camp after learning about this famous Polish activist Lech Walesa. Leo had one reaction—he couldn't believe a kid like Charlie Joe would ever be caught dead at a place like Camp Rituhbukkee.

"Yup," I confirmed to Leo. "I'm on strike."

He whistled into the phone. "Holy smokes. That is totally awesome!"

I smiled. "Yeah, thanks."

"But, like, what about school?"

"Well, here's the thing," I explained. "I'm actually going to need your help, because I still need to do my schoolwork. So you're going to have to get kids to take notes for me and bring me my homework and stuff. You can do it by e-mail, too, if you want."

Leo was silent for a second. I think he had realized he could be considered a co-conspirator if he helped me, and he was trying to decide if that was a good thing or a bad thing.

"I can definitely do that," he said eventually. "Tell me what you need."

Good friends always come through in the clutch.

"Well, the first thing I'm going to need is for you to tell everybody what I'm doing," I said. I imagined the faces on my teachers, and the kids, when Leo started spreading the news. Alex Mutchnik. Cathy Billows. Lucy Fleck. Wow, this was going to be intense. I almost wished I could be there to see it.

"Okay, then what?" Leo asked.

"Then, can you come over after school tomorrow to bring me my homework and stuff?"

"I can't," he sighed. "I have to go to SERVICE."

SERVICE stood for Student Encouraging Relief, Volunteering and Cheering up the Elderly. It was started by Lucy Fleck's older brother Damien—with a lot of help from his mother, I'm sure—as a way for kids to do community work to look good for colleges.

It basically consisted of high school kids getting money from their parents to buy food at fancy stores and delivering it to nursing homes and hospitals in the area. Now the middle school kids were starting to do it, too.

Thank God SERVICE was one activity I didn't have to do, probably because even my dad thought Mrs. Fleck was crazy. Ever since she tried to establish a gifted program in nursery school, he didn't want anything to do with her.

"Okay, cool," I said to Leo. "Maybe after SERVICE you can e-mail me some of the work, cool?"

"Totally cool," he said. "What you're doing is so awesome. I totally wish I had the guts to do it."

I heard the front door open. My heart started thumping.

Dad.

"I better go," I said to Leo. "My dad's home."

"Does he know what you're up to?"

"Not really," I said.

Leo whistled again. "I'll talk to you tomorrow, if you're still alive."

19

I heard my dad put his briefcase on the floor. Then I heard his footsteps. He was coming my way.

Maddie jumped off the couch and left the room. She didn't want any part of what was about to happen. Neither did I, frankly, but I didn't have much choice.

Nana came in first. She always had my back.

Dad was right behind her.

"How was your day?" he said, trying to be nice.

"Awesome."

"Great."

He loosened his tie and rubbed his eyes. Looking at him, it occurred to me how tired he was, how tired he always was, and how hard he worked. I suddenly felt a little guilty for adding more stress to his life.

"You need to stop this nonsense," said my dad.

"I will," I said, "as soon as you let me drop some of my activities."

"That's ridiculous," said my dad.

"You're ridiculous." Something about the last couple of days was making me a little too brave for my own good.

He looked at me like he didn't quite recognize me. "You're not quitting anything."

"Who said anything about quitting?" Nana butted in. "It's not quitting if you stop doing things you never want to do."

"Rose, stay out of this please!" my dad snapped. Nana looked shocked. At first I thought she was going to yell back at him, but then I think she remembered she was living in his house and backed off.

My mom brought my dad a beer, and he took a big swig. "I'll let you quit—sorry, give up—one thing," he offered.

I shook my head. "You don't get it, Dad. I just want to do the stuff I like. I like the cello. In fact, I plan on practicing right here on the couch! And I guess I do like baseball, even though I'm not very good at it. But everything else, forget it."

Dad shook his head slowly. "Well then, I guess we've got nothing else to talk about." He got up. "Have a nice life on the couch."

"Thanks," I said. "I plan on it."

I tried to eavesdrop on my parents and Nana while my dad ate dinner, but they shut the door. Afterward, my parents went upstairs to read and watch TV in their bedroom.

Nana stayed downstairs with me, got me some ice cream, and we played gin rummy, her favorite card game. After a while my mom came back down with my cello. "I heard you say you planned on practicing?"

"Tomorrow."

Mom looked like she was about to leave the room, but then she stopped and turned back.

"You do realize how lucky you are, right?" she said. "How many opportunities you have, and how wonderful your life is, all because of how hard your dad works?"

"And how hard *you* work," Nana said, looking at my mother.

I put down my cards. "I know, Mom."

"There are families who would kill to have what you have," she continued, bending down to look me square in the eye. "Ninety-nine percent of the families in the world, in fact. Please don't ever forget that."

I tried to stare back at her but couldn't quite pull it off. "I won't. I promise."

She kissed the top of my head. "Don't forget to brush your teeth," she said, and headed upstairs.

Nana and I kept playing, but neither of us talked for a while. I think we were both thinking about what my mom had said. She was absolutely right, of course.

But that didn't mean I was wrong.

When I went to the bathroom before bed, I looked around the hall like I'd never seen it before. There was a nice family photo that I looked at for a while. There was a cool painting of a guy fishing. The light had an interesting glow. The houses across the street were interesting if you really stopped to look at them.

Then I peeked up the stairs. I could see the door to my room. I wondered how long it would be before I slept in my own bed again. I was tempted to go up and see if my room looked the same as it did yesterday, but I didn't. That would have been breaking the rules. My rules.

When Nana got up to go to bed, she kissed the top of my head, too.

"Same time tomorrow?" she asked.

I nodded. "I'll be here."

She shook her head. "Oh, boy. This is going to get hairy."

I turned out the lights and went to sleep.

20

STRIKE—DAY 3

The next thing I knew, a bright light was shining in my eyes, and a scary voice was yelling, "Get up!"

I wasn't sure if it was a dream or not. I tried to open one eye. "What time is it?"

"Five o'clock," said the voice, which I was slowly starting to realize was my dad's.

I rubbed my eyes and saw him standing there in his suit and tie. It was still completely dark out, but he'd turned all the lights on in the room. I realized this was when he headed out the door to work every day, and I suddenly felt bad for him.

"Are you waking me up to say goodbye?"

He pushed my legs off the couch and sat down. "No. I'm waking you up to tell you that if you don't go to school today, you'll be grounded for the entire summer."

"Okay."

"Okay, what?"

"Okay, I'll be grounded for the entire summer."

My dad looked like he was about to yell, but he didn't. Instead, he just said quietly, "Jack, you are unbelievable."

My mom came into the room, looking like a zombie.

"What's going on?"

"I'm trying to get it through our son's head that this nonsense has gone on long enough," said my dad.

"Okay, but it's five in the morning, he should be sleeping—"

"STOP UNDERMINING ME!" my dad yelled at

my mom. "I'm trying to take care of this situation. If it were up to you, he'd have a perfectly swell time on the couch the rest of his life!"

"That's not true," said my mom. "I just go about things differently than you."

"You don't go about things at all!" said my dad, still yelling, though not as loudly. "You're too nice! You can't even discipline your own son. Don't you see how much harder that makes it for me?"

It was my mom's turn to raise her voice a bit. "Well, you're the one who's so convinced that Jack has to spend his life running around from thing to thing to thing. This is your mess, you figure it out."

"That's exactly what I'm trying to do!"

"Fine!"

"STOP FIGHTING!" I interrupted, joining the yelling. "I don't want to live on the couch for the rest of my life, obviously! I just want to live a normal life and do the things I want to do! What is wrong with that?"

My dad looked at his watch, mumbled something under his breath, and got off the couch.

"I'm going to miss the train." He stared at my mom. "I want him in school today."

Then he walked out of the room and left the house without kissing her goodbye.

"I'm really sorry, Mom," I said.

She looked at me. "Go back to sleep," was all she said.

21

I fell back asleep, and when I woke up again, Nana was sitting on the couch next to me, watching the morning news.

"What time is it?" I asked for the second time that morning.

"Almost nine," Nana said. "You were out like a light."

"Where's Mom?"

"She had to go to the school and explain what's going on, and then she's going straight to work." My mom volunteered two days a week every June at the local high school, helping kids find summer jobs. "You're causing quite a stir, young man," Nana added.

It took me a second to remember the early-morning fight.

And then it took me another second to realize that my mom hadn't made me go to school after all.

Suddenly I felt really guilty. I hated being the cause of my parents fighting.

"Am I doing the wrong thing, Nana? Should I get up and go to school?"

She sighed. "You're doing a brave thing, Moochie-pooch," she said. (For some reason known only to her, she sometimes called me "Moochie-pooch.") "You're sticking up for what you believe in. But sometimes, doing a brave thing can cause problems."

"I guess so."

So I decided to stick with my strike, at least for one more day. I didn't want to cause problems between my parents. Plus, I was pretty sure that when Dad got home that night, he'd physically remove me from the couch anyway. But even if the strike ended, I felt like I'd made my point. I'd been on the couch for more than two days, and I'd stood up to my dad, which was something to be proud of. And if I did end up going back to school the next day, all the kids would think what I did was cool. That was something to look forward to.

Nana decided that if this was going to be my last day on the couch, we should make it special. So we ordered Chinese food and watched *Dodgeball*. What an amazing movie.

"Ben Stiller is extremely talented," Nana said, even though she thought the movie was a little silly. "Just like his parents." Whoever they were.

In the middle of the movie I got a text from Leo: COMING OVER LATER WITH MARCUS.

I texted back: COOL.

Marcus was Leo's older brother. His main claim to fame was that he had the longest arms of any human being I'd ever known. He was a nice kid, but I had no idea why he was coming over. Either way, it would be good to see Leo. It had been only two days, but I was starting to miss my friends.

After *Dodgeball* ended, I asked Nana if she wanted to put in a yoga DVD.

"Not today, Moochie-pooch."

"Why not?"

"Because I'm taking a walk with Peter." Peter was Nana's friend. Exactly what kind of friend, I didn't know, and I didn't want to find out.

"Fine, be that way," I said as she hugged me good-bye.

Time ticked by kind of slowly. After a while, I looked at the clock. 2:55 p.m. A long time until dinner, Mom wasn't home, I was sick of TV, I didn't feel like reading, and Maddie was snoozing.

I didn't want to admit it, but for the first time in my short couch life, I was bored.

Then the doorbell rang. Thank God.

Technically, I wasn't allowed to answer the door, but I decided to combine it with a bathroom break.

"Dude!" said Leo, who was standing there with his long-armed brother.

"What's up," said Marcus, sounding as though he really didn't care what was up at all.

I closed the door behind them. "Are you guys coming from SERVICE?"

Marcus snorted. "Yup. What a joke."

While I headed to the bathroom, Leo went into the kitchen and helped himself to some chocolate milk, as usual. "Marcus totally agrees with you," he said, between slurps. "He thinks this whole town has gone insane with parents freaking out about what colleges their kids are going to get into."

Leo followed me as I headed back to the couch.

"That's why I wanted him to come over and talk to you about what you're doing." He dumped about a zillion pieces of paper out of his backpack and onto the coffee table. "And I brought you some of your homework, too."

Marcus and I plopped down on the couch at the same time, startling Maddie. She'd been running full speed in her sleep, probably chasing a squirrel.

"So what is this all about?" Marcus asked, opening his eyes to an almost-awake level. "You're seriously, like, sleeping on your couch now?"

"Not just sleeping," I corrected. "Living. I'm living on the couch, and when I say living, I mean LIVING. As in, I'm not getting off the couch ever."

Marcus opened his eyes a bit more. "Huh?"

"I've been overscheduled my whole life, and I've finally had enough," I explained. "Doing dumb activities like learning Chinese and karate and tennis, and having tutors, just because my parents want me to be this high-achieving, well-rounded person. But all it's really done is make me hate that stuff even more."

"So he went on strike," Leo added.

Suddenly Marcus was wide-awake. "So what you're saying is, you're living on your couch because you're protesting against parents locking their kids in the prison of overactivity?"

I hadn't quite thought about it like that, but I nodded anyway.

Marcus started pacing around the room. He jabbed his brother in the ribs. "Get me a piece of paper."

"Ow!" Leo cried, wincing in pain. He rubbed his side. "Why?"

"I might want to write an article for the school newspaper," said Marcus. "I need to take some notes."

"The school newspaper?" I asked. That sounded cool. That sounded like people would pay attention to what I was doing, and think it was interesting, and support me!

Which meant, of course, that I might not be going back to school after all . . . which I would have to tell my dad . . . who was already completely mad at me.

Uh-oh.

Marcus Landis grabbed

a pen and some paper from his brother, sat down next to me, and smacked me in the back. He'd gone from coma to hyper in about seven minutes.

"Tell me everything," he said.

22

My dad tried a new approach when he got home.

He acted like he was my best buddy.

"I totally get what you're doing," he said, sitting down next to me on the couch, munching on a cookie. "I do. You're too busy, you're feeling too much pressure, why should a young kid like you have to worry about looking good for college. I totally get it. Let's figure out how to fix it."

"I know how to fix it," I said. "I want to quit karate and soccer and tennis and Chinese. No more tutors. And no more test-prep classes."

My dad's smile started to look a little forced. "Can I get you a bowl of ice cream while we talk about it?"

"No thanks. I'm having dessert with Nana."

"Honey?" he yelled to my mom. "I need to talk to your mother." I was pretty sure he was going to tell her to stop making my couch life so much fun.

He turned back to me. "How about we

compromise? You can definitely not do the tennis lessons that I just signed you up for."

"Not good enough."

The smile disappeared completely. "Well in any case, you need to go back to school while we figure this out. You can't miss any more school, you'll fall behind."

"Mrs. Bender said she'd send all my work home," I said, referring to my teacher with the tiny mustache.

"She did, did she? Well, I'm going to call her right now."

My dad went into the kitchen, mumbling under his breath. The mumbling got louder when he couldn't find the school phone book. Then the mumbling turned into actual cursing when he couldn't find the phone itself. Finally, he found everything he was looking for, and the cursing became mumbling again.

"Yes, hello, this is Jack Strong's father . . . Yes, nice to speak with you as well . . . It is a strange situation, indeed . . . I just can't have him falling behind on his schoolwork, on top of everything else . . . Yes . . . I see . . . Of course, of course . . . Well, thank you very much for your time."

He marched back into the TV room.

"She says what you're doing is part of the tradition of free speech and expression that makes this country great," he said.

Ah, good old Mrs. Bender.

"Leo's brother Marcus said the same thing," I told my dad. "He thinks I'm doing a great thing, and he's going to write an article about me in the school newspaper."

That was the end of my dad being nice. It was also the end of my dad trying to change my mind.

"Fine," he announced. "It's your life. Stay on that couch forever for all I care. I'm going to eat dinner, do some work, and then take the dog for a walk, and actually live like a normal human being. You should try it sometime." He got up from the couch. "Call me when you're ready to get back to real life. Until then, I'm done." And he walked out of the room.

He passed my mom, who was bringing me dinner.

"He'll calm down," she whispered to me. "He doesn't mean it. Things will be fine in a little while."

But they weren't.

My dad didn't talk to me again for two days.

23

STRIKE—DAY 5

It was Friday morning when things started to get a little crazy.

Leo called first thing in the morning, while I was eating breakfast (on the couch, of course).

"Go to the Inkblots website." *Inkblots* is the name of the high school newspaper.

"Why?" I asked, although I kind of knew. My heart started to pound.

"Just do it," said Leo.

I leaned over to the computer (Nana had moved it next to the couch for easy access) and found the website. I couldn't believe my eyes.

There was an article about me. And it was HUGE.

Horace Henchell Student Takes a Stand by Taking a Seat

By Marcus Landis

Horace Henchell Middle School student Jack Strong has spent his entire life running from one extracurricular activity to another, and now he has finally decided he has had enough.

"I was just tired of doing all this stuff I didn't want to do, that my parents were making me do," said Strong, a seventh grader. "They think I need to do it to get good at everything and look good for college, but I would rather just live like a regular kid and have time for regular kid things like TV, video games, and just hanging around."

This past Monday, after a long weekend of games and practices and recitals and classes, Strong came home from school and was very tired. When his mom tried to get him to go to soccer practice, Strong said he was too tired to go. Then Jack's father got involved, tensions escalated, and Jack announced once and for all that he wasn't going to practice. When Jack's dad asked him, "Do you want to just sit on the couch for the rest of your life and do nothing?" Jack Strong thought about it for a minute, and then answered, YES.

Which is when Jack Strong went on strike.

He's been on the couch for five days so far, and he's decided that he won't get up from the couch until his parents promise to let him drop a bunch of the activities that he doesn't want to do.

"It's not like I'm trying to make a big point or anything," Strong explains. "And I don't expect anybody else to do what I'm doing. It's probably pretty stupid, not going to school and everything. But it's just something I wanted to do, because I felt strongly about it."

Jack now spends his days on the couch exercising and watching TV with his grandmother, reading and doing homework, playing video games and hanging out with his dog, Maddie. The only times he gets up from the couch are to get something to eat and to go to the bathroom.

"I'm not going to lie, sometimes it gets a little boring," said Jack. "But it's a lot more fun than learning how to say the names of various household appliances in Chinese."

Jack Strong's mother and father were unavailable for comment.

I finished the article, and read it again. Then I read it again.

"Leo, are you still there?" I whispered, after the third time.

"Yup."

I let out a long breath. "Holy moly."

"I know. Are your parents going to kill you?"

I shook my head, even though Leo couldn't see me. "My dad is too mad to even talk to me. He's just ignoring me now and waiting for me to get bored and give up. And my mom is making up for my dad being a jerk by being extra nice."

That was true. I'd realized that some part of her was tired of my dad making me do all these activities. And besides, she always reacted to Dad being mad at me by being even nicer than usual. The last couple of days she'd even made all my favorite meals and picked up my homework from school. When I asked her if Dad would be mad at her for doing that, she patted my arm and said, "You just leave that to me."

So I left it to her.

"Well, I gotta go to school," said Leo. "I guess I'll talk to you later?"

"I guess so. Hey did my parents really refuse to comment?"

"Nah. I think he just wrote that because he says that's what reporters write when they're too lazy to actually interview somebody."

"Got it."

We hung up, and I sat back on the couch and closed my eyes. It was dead silent. Dad was at work, my mom had taken Nana to get her heart medicine, and Maddie was outside trying to catch squirrels—she was 0 for 4,647 so far. I was alone in the house. I was getting used to being alone. I'd been on that couch for five days, and even though Mom and Nana were usually around, I'd never been alone so much in my life. But I had a feeling that was about to change.

I was right.

24

At exactly 3:02, the doorbell rang.

"It's open!" I yelled.

Maddie started barking like crazy, and I knew that it wasn't just Leo or somebody else who came over all the time.

"Who's there?" I shouted, but no one answered. Maddie kept barking, and suddenly I had to come up with a way to scare away a burglar while not getting up from the couch.

I was thinking over my strategy when I heard Leo yell, "It's just us!"

Us?

I looked up and saw Leo come into the room. Behind him were Cathy Billows, Baxter Billows, Sam French, Kevin Kessler, Vanessa Cummings, and Jenny Zeilinksy.

"JACK!" Cathy shouted, shoving the high school newspaper into my hand. "You're famous!"

I'd forgotten that the paper was distributed at the middle school, too. The headline was even bigger in print.

"Take a stand by taking a seat," said Sam French, who up until that very moment had been way too cool to ever even look in my direction. "Pretty awesome, dude."

"Completely," agreed Jenny, whose long auburny-red hair had basically declared her off-limits to all but the lucky few. "I totally wish I thought of that."

Leo sat down next to me. "These guys just wanted

to come over and tell you in person how what you're doing is so awesome," he said. "That's okay, right?"

I looked around at all the kids. This was the A-list. The cream of the crop. The future football captains and cheerleaders. The kings and queens of the jungle.

"Yeah, it's great," I said. "Help yourself to anything in the kitchen. I'd get it for you myself, but well, you know."

When they all laughed at that lame joke like I was the funniest guy on the planet, I knew my life had changed forever.

Cathy came up to me. "You don't look so hot, Jack," she said, suddenly concerned about my well-being. "You look like you haven't been outside in a week."

"I haven't," I reminded her.

"Hey, I've got an idea!" announced Kevin Kessler, smacking his forehead just like animals do in cartoons when they have ideas. "We should, like, carry your couch outside!"

"Dude, that's an awesome idea!" cried Sam, smacking his forehead, too, for no apparent reason.

What a couple of goofballs. But here's the thing. It *was* an awesome idea.

In fact, it was such a good idea, I was mad that I hadn't thought of it. Move the couch outside! It was brilliant! That way, I could still be on strike but be in the front yard, get some fresh air, and hang out with people in the neighborhood.

Then again, maybe I hadn't thought of it because the couch was a little too heavy for my grandmother to lift.

I nodded. "Okay, but it's going to be pretty heavy, because I have to stay on it while you move it. We can go through the screen porch because the door is super wide."

"Take all the cushions and pillows off," Leo instructed. Everyone did as they were told, because Leo got really good grades.

Cathy, Leo, and Kevin got on one side of the couch, with Baxter, Jenny, Sam, and Vanessa on the other.

Maddie started barking at them, like she thought it was a bad idea.

"And . . . up!" commanded Baxter.

Together everyone hoisted the couch (and me), and somehow they managed to stagger to the screen porch, just missing about three fancy vases on the way.

"Careful," I said, nervously enjoying the ride.

"Yes, your highness," muttered Leo.

We (okay, they) pushed ahead heroically. I couldn't believe they were going to pull it off! I hadn't been outside in five days.

Then Nana wandered in. "Jack, I'm going to take a quick nap—"

She saw us and almost dropped her juice. "What in the world—?"

"Oh, hi, Mrs. Kellerman!" Leo said, giving her a friendly wave.

He shouldn't have done that.

See, the thing is, you need a hand to wave. Which means, he only had one hand on the couch. Which means, his side suddenly started tilting downward. Which means, the whole delicate balance was thrown off.

Which means, the couch came crashing down on Kevin Kessler's foot.

Kevin yelled "OW!" so loud that Maddie got scared and bolted through the screen door, which unfortunately wasn't open at the time. The screen popped out of the door, went flying backward, and crushed half of my mom's prized rose bushes.

Then Maddie ran over the screen and trampled the other half.

We waited there for a minute to let Kevin work out his pain.

"Are you okay?" Vanessa finally said.

Kevin squinted and said, "Let's get this frickin' thing outside."

Man, football players are tough. Even middle school football players.

Thirty seconds later, I was sitting on the couch in the bright mid-afternoon sun. It was glorious!

Nana followed us outside.

"Are you planning on sleeping out here?" she asked.

I answered with a shrug.

She sat down next to me. "Listen, kiddo, I'm your biggest fan, but I'm not sure about this maneuver."

"I'm on strike, Nana!"

"I know you are, dear," she said. "And I think that's wonderful, as long as you don't break the house."

25

I forgot how awesome outside was.

The sun was shining, the birds were chirping, the trees were rustling, and the coolest kids in the grade were in my yard playing coed touch football, with me as automatic quarterback.

It turns out that coed touch football is really fun, especially when you never have to get up from the couch.

"Hike!" I hollered, standing on the top of the cushions. My receivers, Baxter and Cathy, went out. I saw Baxter streak by Kevin Kessler, who was obviously still a little hampered by the fact that a three-hundred-pound couch had been dropped on his toe.

I threw a somewhat pathetic spiral to Baxter's shoes, but he was so athletic that he grabbed it easily.

"Touchdown!" he screamed, accepting a hug from an auburn-hair-swirling Jenny Zeilinsky. He headed over to me for a high-five, just as my phone rang.

"Dude, you are seriously popular all of a sudden," Baxter said, pointing at my phone.

He had a point. I'd gotten a bunch of phone calls from people who had either read the article, heard about it from other kids, or seen it online.

The weirdest call was from Dr. Steckler, who was my mom's podiatrist. "I wish I'd been brave enough to take a stand against my parents, like you did," Dr. Steckler told me. "I never would have gone to medical school."

That made me think that maybe Mom should get a new podiatrist.

I checked the caller ID. UNKNOWN, it said. Great. More small talk with a stranger.

"Hello?" I said.

"Is this Jack Strong?" said a voice that was immediately familiar.

"Yes?"

"*The* Jack Strong?"

"Do I know you?"

The voice chuckled. "I sure hope so. If not, I'm not doing my job right."

Wait a second. Could it be? It sounded exactly like—no way—

"This is Brody Newhouse."

It was.

Brody Newhouse was a pretty big deal. He was the host of *Kidz in the Newz*, a local TV show that was on every Wednesday night, where he interviewed kids from the area who had done something interesting that got people talking. A lot of people watched it.

"Um, really?" I managed to stammer. "Brody Newhouse?"

He chuckled. "That's right, kid. The one and only.

Hey, listen, part of our job is to keep an eye on all the local school newspapers. When we saw your article, we thought you'd be great for our show."

I couldn't believe what I was hearing. Me, Jack Strong, on TV?

"I don't get it, Mr. Newhouse. Don't you usually have kids on who, like, pull a dog from a burning house or save a drowning lady or something?"

"Call me Brody. And, yes, that's true. Many of our guests have done something brave. But what you're doing is equally courageous. You're standing up for kids everywhere. By sitting down!" Then he laughed that Brody Newhouse laugh that I've heard in my living room about sixty-two thousand times.

"Wow. Um . . . I don't know what to say, Mr. Newhouse."

"It's Brody!"

By now the other kids had realized this was a different kind of phone call than the others, and they all gathered around to try and listen in.

"Brody Newhouse," I silently mouthed to them. "I swear."

"NO WAY!" yelled Kevin Kessler, who had officially forgotten about his wounded toe.

Brody laughed again. "Sounds like you're having a bit of a party there. Celebrating a little bit?"

"Kind of, I guess."

"So here's what I'd like to do," he said, suddenly turning serious. "I'm going to want to come up there and see exactly what's going on. How long have you been on that couch?"

"Five days," I said, suddenly realizing how puny that sounded.

But Brody didn't think so. "Five days on the couch? Holy moly, how have you not gone crazy?"

"Sometimes it gets a little boring, but basically it's been good."

"What do you do all day?"

"Oh, you know, read, watch TV, do some exercises, hang out with my grandmother, stuff like that."

"What about the bathroom?"

"That's the one time I'm allowed to get up. And for food, sometimes."

"And your parents still haven't let you drop any of these activities?"

"My dad is pretty stubborn, I guess."

"And so are you," said Brody Newhouse. Then he whistled. "Son takes on father! Takes a stand by taking a seat! Overscheduled kids unite! This is golden!"

Cathy Billows elbowed me in the ribs. "What's he saying? Is it really him?"

"Sshhh!" I snapped. Wow, I was shushing Cathy Billows. The world was officially upside down.

"My friends can't believe it's really you," I told Brody. "This is so cool."

"Well, tell them it's really me," he said. "And if it's okay by you, I'd like to come by Monday around five."

"My schedule is wide open," I said, which made him howl with laughter.

"I love this kid! I love him!" He put his hand over the phone, but I could still hear him say, "Shaina, I need to be at this Strong kid's house Monday at five. If all goes well and he's the real deal, we'll put him on Wednesday's show." He returned to me. "Okay pal, see you Monday. No friends hanging around, I'm afraid. Just you and me. Don't want a circus."

"Yes, Mr. Newhouse," I said. I could tell he was about to hang up, so I added, "Oh, just one more thing."

"What's that, kid?"

I held out the phone so I could say it just as much to my new friends as I could to Brody Newhouse.

"I'm the real deal."

26

About twenty minutes later, Jenny's and Kevin's moms came to pick up all the kids.

"Thanks for coming by," I said to everyone, but mainly to Cathy.

"No problem, it was really fun," she said. "It's cool hanging out with a celebrity and everything."

"Yeah, sorry we can't move you back inside," Kevin said, "but I'm already late for basketball."

Baxter nodded. "Yup, some of us still have stuff we have to go to," he said, and everyone laughed.

"No problem," I said, but what I was actually thinking was, *How the heck am I going to get back inside?*

The only logical answer—Dad—was also the only impossible answer.

Nana woke up from her nap about a half hour after they all left. She made herself a tongue sandwich and me a meatball sandwich, then joined me on the front lawn. I couldn't wait to tell her the exciting news about Brody Newhouse.

"Who's Brody Newhouse?" Nana asked.

I laughed. "Only the coolest guy on TV."

"My grandson the star," she said, just as my mom pulled into the driveway. She got out of her car and took it all in. Her screen door, her couch, and her son, all in the front yard.

She wasn't exactly thrilled.

"Does someone want to explain to me what's going on, and what happened to my rose bushes?"

Before I could answer, Nana jumped in. "You're son is going to be famous," she said, chomping on her sandwich.

"Oh really," my mom said. "This I gotta hear."

"Okay," I said, relieved.

She sat down next to me. "After you tell me about the screen door."

I was telling my mom the whole story, and was up to the part about playing football in the yard, when I felt the first raindrop. Maddie started barking to get in. She hated rain almost as much as she loved anything edible.

My mom looked up to the sky worriedly. "Mom, have you heard anything about rain?"

Nana was a big fan of watching weather on TV. She nodded. "As a matter of fact, I have. It's supposed to rain quite a bit tonight."

We all looked at one another, and then at the couch that had taken seven strong kids to move outside.

"Fantastic," said my mom. Then she looked at me. "I don't suppose this will make you get up from the couch?"

I raised my arms to the sky. "Are you kidding? What's a little rain when you've got the host of *Kidz in the Newz* coming to your house to talk about putting you on TV?"

"You're lucky I was planning on replacing this ratty old thing anyway," Mom said, shaking her head at the couch. "I'm going to call Dad."

She and Nana took Maddie inside, and a minute later Nana came out with a poncho.

"Are you sure about this, kiddo?"

"I'm sure."

"Well," she said, wrapping the poncho around me, "you're a better man than I."

27

The next two hours were probably the wettest of my life. They were pretty miserable, too.

And I would say that I thought about giving up my strike and going inside, oh, somewhere around 643 times.

But I didn't. I stayed there. For some crazy reason, I stayed. A crazy reason that was some combination of Cathy Billows, Brody Newhouse, and the fact that I actually believed in what I was doing.

Luckily for me, it wasn't cold, or else I probably would have gotten pneumonia and died before the big TV show.

At one point, my mom came out and gave me soup. At another point, Nana came out and gave me hot cider.

I looked at her. "You guys do know it's not winter, right?"

"Well, you can't be too careful," Nana said.

The cider was delicious.

It started raining harder.

Maddie stood at the window, staring at me like I was crazy.

She had a good point.

I had nothing to do because I couldn't use my cell phone in the rain, I couldn't read in the rain, and I sure couldn't watch TV in the rain. I started to understand why the contestants on *Now What?!?* were so miserable. The only thing to do was to curse Kevin Kessler and his stupid idea to move the couch outside, even though four hours earlier, it had been like the best idea ever.

So I hunkered down in my poncho, sipped my cider, and stared at the gray sky.

Eventually, I got up off the couch and headed inside to use the bathroom. As I stared at myself in the mirror—a wet mess—I couldn't believe how much had changed. In five days, I'd gone from a pretty normal, somewhat invisible, typically overscheduled kid to a mini-celebrity, local hero, and determined but soggy crusader.

Would it be worth it?

I had no idea.

By the time my dad pulled into the driveway, it was pouring so hard he couldn't even see me when he got out of the car.

He was halfway up the front steps when he saw his only son sitting in the front yard, on a couch, in a rainstorm.

He stopped and stood there, his suit soaking in the rain. Then he came over to me and said the first words he'd said to me in two days.

"Better bundle up."

And he went inside and had dinner.

An hour and a half later, it had gotten pitch black and was still raining. Then the porch light came on, the screen door opened, and my dad came outside with a flashlight. He walked up and stood over me.

"Did you know that I was the first member of my family to go to college?"

"Yup," I answered. He'd told me that a lot. Usually when he was trying to talk me into doing something that was good for college.

"What I bet you didn't know," he said, "was that I didn't want to go."

I squinted into the blinding flashlight but didn't say anything.

"My dad owned a kitchen supply store," Dad continued. "It was pretty tiny, but it got us by. I worked there every summer from the age of eleven. I actually loved it. I thought for sure he was going to hand the store down to me. And when I was in high school, and he got sick"—my dad stopped for a minute, the way he always did when he talked about his dad getting sick—"I told him I wanted to take over the store right after I graduated. I knew if I didn't take over, he was going to have to sell it. Which was a big deal, because the store had been his dad's store, and his dad's dad's store before that."

The flashlight suddenly went out, and my dad started fiddling with it. "Dang battery," he muttered.

"So what happened with your dad?" I asked him in the dark.

"Well, we got in a pretty big fight, is what happened. My dad told me there was no way I wasn't going to college. I told him there was no way I was. We screamed at each other all night. We were both incredibly stubborn, I guess. Sounds familiar, right?"

He stopped, like he was actually waiting for an answer, so I said, "Right."

"I didn't realize, of course, just how sick he was. On the day after I graduated from high school, I went down to the store just like always. But it was boarded up. There was a big sign on the door that said SOLD."

Then my dad sat down on the couch next to me.

"He died a year later. My mom told me much later on that the sale of the store paid for the first two years of college, and his life insurance paid for the rest."

The flashlight suddenly came back on, and I was able to see his face. It was wet. I think with rain.

"I wish I'd gotten to know him," I said softly. "He sounds pretty awesome."

"He was," my dad answered, after a minute. "Even though he used to drive me crazy a lot."

We sat there for a minute, just listening to the rain slow to a drizzle.

"People are paying attention to me," I said to my dad. "Kids are noticing. Kids want to go on strike just like me! How awesome is that? How can I go back to the way it was before?"

I waited for his answer, but there was none.

"And besides," I added, "you still haven't told me I can quit tennis and karate and stop going to tutors." I looked up at him, finally. "Sorry, Dad."

He shined the flashlight up into the sky. "Looks like the rain stopped. Good night." Five minutes later, my mom called me in for a bathroom break. I changed into my pajamas and got a warm blanket. Then I went back outside, lay back down on the wet couch, and thought about what my dad said until I fell asleep.

The next morning when I woke up, the couch and me were somehow back in the TV room. My dad was sitting in a chair next to me, watching SportsCenter.

"How did you get me back in here?" I asked.

"You're a good sleeper" was all he said as he left the room.

28

STRIKE—DAY 6

On Saturday, for the first time since the strike began, I felt like playing the cello. I'd been practicing for about an hour and a half when my cell phone rang.

"Hello?"

"Jack? It's Lucy Fleck."

She was whispering for some reason.

"Hey, Lucy. What's up?"

"I wanted to check in with you to make sure you were well."

"Really?"

"Yeah." She lowered her voice even further, to a level only dogs could hear. "Are you?"

"I'm good," I told Lucy.

"I think what you're doing is extreme," she said, "but I admire your perseverance."

"Thanks."

"I can imagine your father is quite upset with you."

Now it was my turn to whisper, since he was in the next room. "My dad freaked out when I told him. He's still freaked out. But you know what? The world didn't end. I'm still here. Not to mention the fact that Brody Newhouse is coming over on Monday."

"WHAT?!?" Lucy shouted. "I mean, what?!?" she repeated, returning to a whisper.

"It's true."

"I imagine there's a story behind that bit of news."

"There is." And I told her the whole story: about the kids coming over, the toe injury, the touch football game, the phone call from Brody, and sleeping in the rain. Afterward, I waited for her to congratulate me and tell me how awesome it was that I was going to be on a popular TV show about brave kids.

But the only thing she said was "Baxter Billows was at your house? That's interesting."

"Why, do you like him?"

"Don't be ridiculous," she said, but I could almost feel her blushing.

"Okay, sorry."

"I have to go," she said. And she hung up.

I guess deep down, girls are all the same.

Even piano-playing, fencing, ice-skating girls.

29

There's not much to report from the rest of the weekend. I spent most of my time waiting for Monday and the meeting with Brody.

On Saturday afternoon, Leo came over to play video games. After about fifteen minutes, I told him that video games are a lot less fun when you can play them whenever you want.

"That's impossible," Leo said.

"Trust me," I told him.

We ended up just hanging out and talking about Cathy Billows and her adorable lack of ability at touch football. (Well, I talked, and Leo shook his head and rolled his eyes.)

On Saturday night, Mom, Dad, and Nana went out to dinner.

"Do you want to come?" Mom asked.

"Can the couch fit in the car?" I answered.

They brought me back a doggie bag.

On Sunday morning, Nana baked an amazing batch of chocolate chip cookies, maybe her best batch ever, and then proceeded to give me only three of them.

"Are you serious?" I cried. "What are you doing with the rest?"

"Giving them to your principal and your teachers, to thank them for not kicking you out of school," she said.

On Sunday afternoon, I texted Charlie Joe Jackson and told him everything. He texted me back a one-word answer: JEALOUS.

Two minutes later, he texted me again: I KNEW YOU COULD DO IT.

On Sunday night, Cathy Billows instant-messaged me for the first time ever.

HAVE FUN TOMORROW! she wrote. TELL BRODY I SAY HI!

I printed it out and had Nana put it in my desk.

I should probably mention one other thing that happened that weekend. Me and my dad went back to not talking to each other.

30

STRIKE—DAY 8

Early Monday morning, my dad came in and woke me up.

"I'm going out of town for two days. Business trip," he told me. "Been scheduled for a while."

I rubbed my eyes but didn't look at him. "Okay."

"Mom told me about this TV guy who's coming to talk to you today."

"Brody Newhouse. He has a show everyone watches. He might want to put me on Wednesday night."

My dad stared down at me. "Why would you assume I would let this happen?"

So here it was, finally. My dad waited and waited—after I told everyone I knew about the TV show—and now, at the last minute, he was going to cancel the whole thing.

"I have no idea," I said, waiting for the ax to fall.

Finally my dad let out a big sigh.

"You can meet the guy," he said. "We'll talk later about the rest of it." He took a deep breath. "You have your assignments for this week?"

"Mrs. Bender sent me everything," I said, still not quite believing that my dad was going to maybe let me go on TV and talk about the strike.

My dad picked up his briefcase. "Just make sure that whatever you tell him, you don't say anything bad about our family," he said. "Never say anything bad about your family. We stick together through thick and thin."

"Okay," I said.

My dad closed his eyes tight for a second, then opened them. "I know I haven't dealt with this in the best way. I know the easy thing to do is just to say fine, go do what you want to do, but I'm not prepared to do that just yet. I don't want you to think you can just pull this stunt and then suddenly get your way about everything. What kind of message would that send?"

He sat down on the couch next to me. "But I've been thinking about things, Jack, and I know we'll be able to figure all this out on Wednesday when I get back." He actually tried to smile a little. "And I'm pretty sure I know where to find you."

Then he kissed me on the top of my head and was gone.

Later that morning, I asked my mom how she got my dad to go along with the whole TV show thing.

"Well, because I told him we should be proud of your bravery and your ability to stand up for something you believe in, and everyone should know it," she said.

I looked at her. "No, really."

My mom winked.

"I told him it would be good for college," she said.

31

Brody Newhouse was an hour late.

"Those show-business types are all the same," Nana said, as we killed time by playing gin rummy. "They only think of themselves. No respect for other people."

"I beg to differ," said a familiar voice, and Nana and I turned around to see the one and only Brody Newhouse walking into the room. Right behind him was my mom, who had a star-struck expression on her face.

Nana and I stared, both of us unable to speak. I'm not even sure I was breathing. It was the first time I'd seen a famous person up close, and I wasn't handling it well.

Brody went straight up to my grandmother. "Who is this gorgeous lady?" he said, kissing her hand.

Suddenly Nana wasn't so mad about the whole Brody-being-late thing.

"Rose Kellerman," she said, doing a little bow, as if Brody were the king of England. "A pleasure to meet you."

"The pleasure is all mine, truly," said Brody. Nana sat down, a little wobbly. For a second it literally looked as if she were going to faint. I think she thought Brody was more famous than he actually was.

"Are you okay, Mom?" asked my mom, concerned.

"I'm fine," said Nana, fanning herself with a magazine. "Absolutely fine. Just overcome with a bad case of celebrity-itis."

Brody laughed, then turned to me. "The man of the hour."

"Hey," I said, extending my hand. He waited for a second as if he thought I wasn't finished, until he realized I wasn't able to come up with anything else to say.

"Hey, yourself," Brody said finally. "It's a real honor to meet you. Seriously, kid, I love what you're doing."

"Don't let his father hear you say that," said my mom. Brody laughed again. The man had unbelievably white teeth.

"So listen, everyone, I brought a few people that I want you to meet. Is it okay if they come in?"

"Sure," my mom said. Brody whipped out his cell phone. "It's a go," he said, then hung up abruptly. "Just some folks that will help us make this story fly," he explained to us. "Always good to build a little momentum before the show airs."

A few seconds later, two men and a woman came in. One of the guys had a video camera, and the other was carrying a massive light. The woman had a microphone, a mirror, and the most well-brushed hair I'd ever seen.

"Hi, Jack!" she said, smiling and showing off her perfect dimples. "I'm Shaina Townsend. I do pieces for the network's website, and I'd love to do a piece on you."

I looked at this really pretty person who was interested in me. "What's 'a piece'?"

She laughed. "A video feature."

Nana marched up to Shaina. "I don't like the news coverage on your channel," she scolded. "It's sensationalist and inflammatory." Then she examined Shaina's face carefully. "But your lipstick is wonderful."

As the two of them became best pals, Brody came and sat next to me on the couch.

"So, here's how it works," he said. "We'd like to do the show Wednesday night. Now as I think you know, we always broadcast live, from the kid's house. So we'll be talking to you on camera in front of a lot of people. I'm not going to lie; it can be pretty intense. Are you sure you can handle that?"

"Honey, I don't know about this," my mom said.

I tried not to let them see me gulp. "No, it's totally fine."

"You'll do great," Brody reassured me. "But it's not all live. That's why we're here today, to do a taped interview with you. There's no big intro here, no big set-up, just some questions. Should be nice and easy." He pointed at the guys with the camera and light, setting up their equipment. "Don't pay any attention to them. Just look right at me."

I looked around the room, trying to convince myself to relax. This was going to be great. I was a hero to kids everywhere! Cathy Billows was my new best friend! Who wouldn't want to trade places with me?

Then the bright lights turned on, the camera's red

light flashed, and Brody smiled the brightest smile I'd ever seen in my life.

"So let me ask you something, Jack," he said. "We did a little background work over the weekend and talked to some other people in town. A lot of people, especially kids, support what you're doing. But we found a number of parents, in particular a woman named Missy Fleck, who seem to feel that what you're doing is extremely dangerous. What do you say to those people?"

A bead of sweat popped out on my forehead. I wasn't sure I heard him right. Why was he talking to

Mrs. Fleck? What did she have to do with this? Wasn't this about me being a hero?

I didn't know what to say, so I just said, "What?"

Before Brody could say anything more, Nana came storming over. "I heard that," she snapped. "What kind of question is that? How dare you put my grandson on the spot like that?"

"Sorry, Mrs . . ."

"Kellerman."

"Sorry, Mrs. Kellerman. But it's important for us to tell all sides of the story. Mrs. Fleck told us point-blank that she's determined to fight back on this issue, that parents need to do whatever they can to make sure their children succeed."

I looked at my grandmother. She had always been a fair person, all for free speech, and she loved a good argument. I saw her anger melt away just a little bit.

"So you've talked to this woman, Mrs. Fleck?"

"Not me personally," said Brody.

"Who then?" Nana demanded.

"I did," Shaina said, walking over to us. "I posted her comments on the website this afternoon."

"Tell them the rest," Brody said.

Shaina's eyes shined with excitement. "When I told Mrs. Fleck that we might do a show about you, she was shocked. She said there's nothing newsworthy about a kid lying on the couch all day."

Then Brody jumped in. "She also said that if the show happened, she'd hold a rally right across the street in protest. During the show."

My stomach did a somersault.

This time it was my mom who stormed over and got in Brody's face. "Are you kidding me? Can she do that? Is that legal?"

"Completely legal, as long as she has a permit," said the camera guy, who didn't want to miss the fun.

My mom threw up her hands. "I'm not sure this is going to work out."

"Mom!" I protested.

"I'm sorry, I can't have a circus going on here," she said. "I'm going to call your father and see what he has to say."

As my mom stormed out of the room—there was a lot of storming going on—everyone started talking at once. For some reason, watching everybody else freak out made me feel calmer.

"I'll answer the question," I said to Brody, and suddenly everyone got really quiet.

"You will?" Brody asked.

"Yes." I shifted in my seat. "I'm sure Mrs. Fleck loves her kids very much. And her daughter, Lucy, is really amazing at a lot of different things."

"Great," said Brody. "That's a cut." The lighting guy turned off his giant light.

"I'm not finished," I said. The guy turned the light back on.

"But here's the thing," I continued, looking at Brody again. "I think Mrs. Fleck pushes her kids too hard. A lot of parents push their kids too hard, and make their kids do too much. And it's wrong."

Then I looked directly into the camera.

"*That's* a cut."

The rest of the interview was pretty quick. Brody asked me about my parents, and I remembered what my dad said about not saying anything bad. So I told him that basically we were a really happy family, even though we disagreed about some things.

"I'll say," Brody said.

"We love each other to death!" Nana shouted from the other room.

Eventually Brody said, "I think I've got everything I need for tonight."

I was confused. "That's it? You're not going to ask me anything about the strike, or my daily schedule, stuff like that?"

Brody shook his head. "Nah, we'll save that stuff for the live broadcast."

I looked at him. "So we're on for Wednesday?"

He smiled that TV smile. "As long as your parents don't shut us down, we're on for Wednesday."

I couldn't believe it. I was actually going to be on TV!

Shaina came over. "Jack, I need to get you on camera to do a teaser for the live show." She sat down next to me as the equipment guys turned their stuff back on.

"Hi, this is Shaina Townsend. I'm here with Jack Strong, the middle school student who's taking a stand by taking a seat," she said. "He's tired of his over-scheduled life, so he's decided to go on strike. He's been sitting on this very couch for a week straight." Then she turned to me. "Jack, tell me something: How long do you think your strike will go on?"

"I'm not sure," I said. "Hopefully not too much longer. Believe it or not, I actually miss school."

Shaina laughed louder than necessary. "And do you think what you're doing will change anything? Will parents understand that it's time to let kids be kids? Will they stop trying to turn them into high-achievement machines programmed for the college application process?"

I thought for a second, trying to figure out how to answer, when I saw my mom walk back into the room. We all stopped and looked at her.

"Are we good?" Brody asked.

My mom sighed. "Yup," she said. "We're good. Richard seems to think the TV show is just what this family needs."

"Yes!" I screamed, nearly jumping off the couch. My dad must have really bought into this whole it-would-be-good-for-college thing. But I suddenly felt guilty because I realized there was no way he wasn't going to look like the bad guy. On live television.

Nana came over and hugged me, then said something about having only two days to find a new dress.

"Jack?" Shaina said. "Back to the question. What

do you think? Will parents understand it's time to let kids be kids?"

"I'm not sure," I said. "You'll have to ask them."

"Ask who?" said Shaina. "The parents or the kids?"

"That's for Wednesday night," interrupted Brody, signaling to his crew to start packing up. "Like I said, gotta save the good stuff for live television."

32

After everyone left, Mom, Nana, and I checked out the network's website. Sure enough, right there on the home page was a big picture of Mrs. Fleck, with the headline: "Local Mom Fights Back."

Missy Fleck, 42, has always considered herself an excellent mother: passionate, hardworking, and extremely dedicated to her children. But suddenly parents like Mrs. Fleck, who shuttle their kids from activity to activity all week long, are under increased scrutiny. This is mostly due to Jack Strong, the middle school student who has gained a great deal of attention in the last week by deciding to go on strike until his parents lighten his own schedule. His motto, TAKE A STAND BY TAKING A SEAT, has become a rallying cry for overscheduled children. But now

Mrs. Fleck, whose daughter goes to school with young Jack, has decided to fight back.

"Jack Strong may be sitting down," Mrs. Fleck said in an interview earlier today, "but I need to stand up for hard-working kids and parents everywhere."

My mom shook her head. "What is happening to the world?"

"This is what happens when you don't let me skip soccer practice," I said.

We kept reading. Sure enough, Mrs. Fleck had decided to hold her own rally right on my street, the night of the live broadcast. "We're going to have music, games, a display of artwork, and much more, all performed and created by the kids," Mrs. Fleck said in the article. "And all made possible by the many wonderful activities they attend and love."

The rest of the article was all the predictable stuff about how Mrs. Fleck is doing all this because she's a champion for children. Whatever. Basically I just skimmed it, until a paragraph at the end caught my eye.

And what do Mrs. Fleck's own children think of this controversy? "She definitely loves us, and has our best interests at heart," says daughter Lucy. "Working hard and doing all these things will help me get into a good college and have a better chance to succeed in life."

Then Mrs. Fleck ended the interview, saying her young daughter was late for her chemistry tutor.

"Most kids don't take chemistry until tenth grade," she said, smiling proudly.

Aha! The real Mrs. Fleck pops up, if only for a minute.

I felt a hand on my shoulder. "Time to wash your hands for dinner," said my mom.

Heading to the bathroom, I was a little wobbly as usual. The first steps when I got up were always weird, like I was just learning how to walk. My legs felt rubbery, and as I looked around, it seemed like I was really high off the ground.

Walking is a really strange thing to do when you only take about fifty steps a day.

In the bathroom, I looked at myself in the mirror. I still looked the same, but everything else about me was different. Last Monday I was just a regular kid trying to survive middle school. Now here I was, about to go on television while a crazy lady was throwing a party dedicated to tearing me down.

What a difference a week makes.

33

STRIKE—DAY 9

So it turns out that being a celebrity is really weird.

It started the day after the article appeared on the internet. First, a few people drove by and took pictures of the house. Then, people started knocking on the door and asking if they could sit next to me on the couch and take a picture together. When one guy snuck around the back and started taking my picture through the window while I was napping, Nana sent him on his way with a few choice words.

I was also interviewed over the phone by some of the other local radio and television stations. Fred's Furniture Farm delivered a new couch to our house, but my mom didn't like it and sent it back. I mentioned Xbox in one interview, and two hours later a brand new system arrived, with a note that said "I want your life!" Luckily it was from an anonymous person, so my mom couldn't send it back, too.

It was official: I was kind of famous. But the strangest part was, even though everybody suddenly wanted a piece of me, I was starting to feel really alone.

First of all, I was starting to realize that when you're the only *under*scheduled kid in a world of *over*scheduled kids, you don't get a lot of company.

And the other thing was, Nana had gone to stay with her friend Lena in the city for a twenty-four-hour bridge binge. She did that twice a year. I think it was kind of like one of those rock festivals, but instead of a bunch of twenty-five-year-olds acting crazy and doing who-knows-what, you had a bunch of seventy-something-year-olds playing bridge and eating cake.

"I'll be back in time for the big show tomorrow night," she told me before she left. "Don't get up from that darn couch before I get back."

I really missed her.

Then, on Tuesday afternoon, while I was tossing apple slices to Maddie (she loves apples), I heard a knock on the window. I turned around, and Leo was standing there on his bicycle.

"Don't worry, I'll let myself in," he said, coming in through the just-fixed screen door.

"Dude!" I pounded his back.

"I'm heading to the store to get my mom a thing of milk," Leo said. "Figured I'd stop here on the way and make sure you weren't too exhausted from not doing anything all day."

"Very funny. You try sitting on a couch for nine days. It's starting to kind of stink."

"Dude, you're famous. That doesn't stink." Then Leo went over to my computer. "But here's the real reason I came over," he said. "My brother showed this to me. Have you heard about this?"

I looked at the screen, which he'd opened to Facebook. Someone had started a page called "The

Sit-Downers." It was for people who wanted to support me in the strike. And it had 1,374 likes!

"Holy moly," I said.

"That's nothing," Leo said, typing on the keyboard. "Check this out."

He clicked on a YouTube video called *Lacey Takes a Stand*.

I pressed play.

It was a video of a girl walking on a beach. She looked a little older than me. She stared into the camera and started talking.

"My name is Lacey Allen. I read about Jack Strong, and his life sounded exactly like my life. I was running from thing to thing, and never had any time to myself. I figured if he was brave enough to finally do something about it, so could I. Except, since I live in California, I figured I could have a couch with a view."

Then she walked up to a couch that was sitting right on the edge of the ocean and sat down. As the camera swung around to the other side, she blew it a kiss.

"Thank you, Jack Strong. I think you're awesome. Bye!"

Then a big frame came up that said "A Lacey Allen Production."

The whole thing was about thirty seconds long. And it had 7,375 views and 284 comments!

"Holy double moly," I said.

"I know!" Leo said, pounding my back.

Wow. This was at a whole new level. People all over the country were starting to do what I was doing. Kids were fighting back against their parents. They were *following me.*

Then the weirdest thing happened. I started to cry. I have no idea why, and just a little, I swear.

Leo stared at me. "Are you okay?"

I wanted to tell him, yeah, I was okay. I was better than okay. I was awesome. I was the luckiest person in the world. I was Jack Strong, who used to be just another kid at Horace Henchell Middle School, but who was now being talked about by cute older girls in California. I was better than okay. I was freakin' great!!

But all I said was, "Yeah, I'm good."

34

STRIKE—DAY 10

The day of the show, I woke up ridiculously early and couldn't get back to sleep. I checked my phone. There were good-luck texts from Cathy, Baxter, and Kevin Kessler. (All kids who barely knew my number a week ago, btw.)

And three missed calls from Lucy Fleck.

I tried to call her back, but it went to voicemail. No doubt she was doing her early morning studying.

I was practicing downward dog on the couch when my mom came in and sat in my dad's favorite chair. The one he used to sit in when he watched TV with my mom, before I took over the room.

"You're getting so good at yoga," she said.

"Usually I do it with Nana, but she's not back from the city yet."

"Right."

My mom picked up a magazine and pretended to read. "Tonight's the big night," she said. I noticed how tired she looked and suddenly realized I hadn't talked to her—I mean, REALLY talked to her—since the whole craziness began.

"Mom?"

She looked up. "Yes, honey?"

"Is everything good with you and Dad?"

"Everything's just fine, honey."

"That's good." I wanted to keep talking, for some reason. "Do you think Dad is going to, like, hate me forever?"

She put down her magazine. "Jack, you do know your dad loves you more than anything in the world, right?"

"Of course I do."

"But this is not easy for him," my mom said. "He has very, very strong beliefs about how to best raise his only child. And now, he's embarrassed on top of it. He's becoming known, completely unfairly, as a crazy dad. People are starting to look at him funny, and people at work are poking fun at him. This is not easy for him, you have to know that."

"I totally know that." After another second, I asked, "But why can't he just let me quit some stuff? Why is that so impossible?"

"Because he's your father," my mom answered.

I changed to the warrior position. Nana would have been totally impressed. "Well, what do *you* think?" I asked my mom.

My mom sighed. "I think you're *both* crazy."

I laughed. "That makes sense."

"I just hope I didn't make a dumb decision by letting this TV show happen," she said. "But maybe we need something crazy like this to help us figure things out."

"Right."

My mom got up. "I need to go pick up your grand-mother at the station."

I decided to ask the question I'd been thinking about for the last two days.

"When is Dad going to be home?"

My mom stopped and looked at me. "I don't know if he's going to make it home tonight, honey. His meet-ings in Phoenix are still going on."

"Oh," I said. For some reason, I was disappointed.

My mom could tell, of course, because that's what

moms do. "But he'll be home tomorrow," she said, "and everything will be okay. That's a promise."

As she started to walk away, I found myself pulling her back toward the couch and giving her a hug.

"What's that for?" she asked, surprised.

I looked up at her. "I guess just for understanding," I said.

My mom hugged me back, and neither one of us said anything for a minute. Finally she let me go.

"If only you were this dedicated to Chinese," she said.

35

At four o'clock, two huge trucks rumbled up our little street and parked on our lawn.

"Whoa," said Nana, peering out the window. After getting home from the city, she'd spent most of the afternoon picking out an outfit.

I'd spent most of the afternoon practicing my answers to imaginary questions.

"Yes, Brody, it's great to be an inspiration to kids around the country."

"Yes, Brody, I do miss school, and my friends, but it's for a good cause."

"No, Brody, I don't have a girlfriend right now, but I'm definitely open to suggestions."

When I heard the roar of the trucks, I looked out the window. A huge guy with a beard hopped out of the first truck.

"Let's set up the stage right here," he yelled to the rest of the guys.

Stage?

"Use the house as the backdrop," he continued. "And get that tree in the frame, too. It's pretty."

Soon, eight more guys jumped out of the trucks. Half of them set up a little path of metal sheets, and the rest unhitched the huge truck doors and started rolling off a bunch of giant steel planks.

The next thing I knew, my mom was running outside at a full sprint.

"Excuse me, excuse me! Hello? What is all this??!?" she yelled at no one in particular.

When no one in particular answered her, she went up to the huge bearded guy, who seemed like he was in charge.

"Can you please move these trucks? You're ruining my lawn."

"Sorry, ma'am, we need to unload the deck for the stage."

"STAGE?!"

The huge bearded guy looked down at her. "Are you Mrs. Strong?"

"Yes," she said. "Get these trucks off my lawn."

"I'd love to, but I'd get fired," he answered.

"Ha-ha," said my mom. "What's your name?"

"Larry," he said a bit reluctantly.

"Well, Larry, this is a TV show, not Woodstock. No one said anything to me about trashing my property. So I suggest you move these trucks in the next five minutes or this whole show isn't going to happen, and then I bet a lot more people will get fired."

Larry examined my mom and quickly decided she wasn't kidding.

"Give me ten minutes."

My mom looked him up and down, then nodded once. "Fine. But if you boys disturb so much as a single dandelion, your lawyers will be hearing from me." Then she gave him a friendly smile. "I'll have some lemonade out in a minute."

As my mom came back inside, she noticed me. "The things mothers do for their children," she said.

Larry the Beard watched her go, then hollered, "Let's pick up the pace, boys!"

Sure enough, exactly ten minutes later the trucks were backing off the lawn and heading up the street to the cul-de-sac.

While the rest of the guys were building the stage,

Larry saw me looking out the window and came over. "That your mom?"

"Yup."

He shook his head. "Piece of work."

"Hey, watch it!" I said.

"It's a compliment, little man," he said, chuckling. "So you're Jack Strong."

"Yup," I said again.

"Cool," Larry said. "Wait here."

"Where am I gonna go?" I said, and he laughed.

A minute later, he came back with three guys, and they picked up my couch and carried me out to the front lawn in about six seconds. And nobody dropped anything on their toes.

"So what's this all about?" Larry asked me, taking a mashed banana out of his jean jacket and eating it.

"What's what all about?"

"This whole strike thing. You trying to get a girl or something?"

"I'm in middle school," I said. "I'm always trying to get a girl."

Larry roared with laughter, little banana particles flying out of his mouth. "That's funny, little man!"

A loud engine got us both to turn around. A huge

trailer was coming up the street, followed by one of those fancy SUVs. They both pulled into our driveway.

I was starting to realize that it takes a lot of vehicles to put on a television show.

"Walter Cronkite's here," Larry said, which I think was some kind of joke that I didn't get.

Brody hopped out of the SUV.

"My guy Jack Strong!" he said, walking up to me and extending his hand. He looked perfect, as usual, except for the fact that he was wearing a bib.

"Hey, Brody," I said.

He pointed at the trailer. "That's where I'll be for the next couple of hours, getting beautiful."

"Cool," I said. Shaina Townsend, the woman who did the background interview with me two days ago, was there, too, wearing the shortest dress I had ever seen. She looked at Brody and smiled, and he looked at her and he smiled, and I immediately decided that they were boyfriend and girlfriend.

Brody turned back to me. "So, we are going to have some fun tonight! Especially with Mrs. Fleck right across the street throwing her own little shindig. Holy smokes, this might be a first, even for me!"

He slapped me on the back and disappeared into the trailer.

Sitting there watching the huge stage being built, I decided to take a picture and text it to Leo.

OMG IT'S HAPPENING.

Two seconds later he texted back.

DOUBLE OMG.

36

The next three hours went by in a blur.

5:00 p.m. A short guy in one of those Crocodile Hunter jackets introduced himself to me. "I'm Mel, Brody's producer," he explained.

I shook his hand. "Nice to meet you."

"We are going to kill it tonight," said Mel, whatever that means.

6:00 p.m. Mrs. Fleck drove past our house and up to the cul-de-sac at the end of the street. The first thing she did was put up a huge poster between two trees. It had a picture of an overweight kid sleeping on a couch and it said, *It's Wrong to Lie*, which was kind of clever, I had to admit.

6:15 p.m. People started joining Mrs. Fleck. I recognized a couple of the stricter teachers from school, a couple of parents and their hopefully unwilling children, and my standardized-test tutor.

(He probably figured he had to support Mrs. Fleck, since it's people like her that helped him put a pool in at his house.)

6:30 p.m. A bunch of kids from school came over to our house, cheering and yelling and holding up signs that said things like *Jack Makes Us All Strong!* and *My Schedule Includes Xbox!* Nana and my mom fed them all pizza. I was too nervous to eat. Which was a first.

6:45 p.m. People kept coming. Some I recognized, some I didn't.

7:00 p.m. A student string quartet started playing Beethoven in the cul-de-sac. Mrs. Fleck cheered as if they were Lady Gaga. The cello player wasn't as good as me. Just saying.

7:30 p.m. The stage was finally ready. There were three cameras. Brody emerged from his trailer and brought a woman over to me to put some makeup on my face. It itched.

7:45 p.m. The couch was lifted up onto the stage, with me on it.

7:50 p.m. The lights came on.

7:59 p.m. Brody looked at me. "You ready, kid?" I nodded. He pointed at the camera. "When you see that red light go on it means we're on the air." He chuckled. "So don't be picking your nose or anything." I responded to that the only way I knew how—by touching my nose. Sweat beads started popping out on my forehead. Brody cracked his knuckles, stretched out his neck, and gave me a thumbs-up. "It's show time."

8:00 p.m.   Show time.

37

A blinding light suddenly zapped me right between the eyes.

Two huge applause signs started blinking, and people in the front yard started clapping and hooting wildly. It was like one of those pregame college football shows on ESPN.

Not everyone clapped, though. Some people actually booed. I should have known right then that things wouldn't go exactly as planned.

The camera panned over the crowd and landed on Brody's bright, toothy smile.

"Hello, everyone, and welcome to *Kidz in the Newz*, the show that brings our area's youngest newsmakers right into your living room. I'm Brody Newhouse, and tonight we're broadcasting live from the front yard of a young man named Jack Strong."

The red light of my camera came on, and I tried to smile. The crowd cheered, and I heard Nana yell,

"Bravo! Bravo!" which made me turn the color of a tomato.

"There's a real problem in this country," Brody continued. "Because the world has gotten so much more competitive, parents have decided that the only way their kids will succeed is by getting into the very best college. And the only way to do that, apparently, is by filling their children's every waking hour with some sort of self-improvement activity, as early as grade school. From sports, to music, to academics, to languages, it's not enough to just be good anymore. Now, you have to be the best. And to be the best, you have to be practicing, working all the time."

Brody turned to another camera. "It was only a matter of time before one of these overscheduled children would decide that they'd had enough. And ten days ago, it finally happened. On a Monday afternoon, after a weekend filled with games, lessons, classes, and tutors, a middle school boy named Jack Strong asked his parents if he could skip soccer practice. They said no. And that was it. That was the last straw for young Jack. He went on strike. He sat down on the couch. He hasn't gotten up since. And now, kids everywhere are supporting him in what's becoming a real movement."

The crowd roared again, until Brody asked for silence.

"But, like any controversial issue, there are passionate arguments on both sides. As we speak, a hundred yards away from us, there is a block party going on sponsored by Missy Fleck, a local parent who has emerged as the most vocal opponent of Jack Strong and what he's doing. She is very firm in her belief that kids need to work hard to get ahead, and there are many that agree with her."

A cheer went up across the street.

"We will be hearing from Mrs. Fleck later," Brody said.

We will?

"As well as a surprise guest," Brody continued.

Really? Who? For a second I thought *Dad?*

"And in a moment," Brody concluded, "we will hear from the man himself, Jack Strong. But first, a little background on this amazing story."

The lights went out as a bunch of screens set up around the yard played a short report narrated by Shaina Townsend. There were pictures of me doing all my various activities. There was an interview with Mrs. Bender at school, where she called me "one of her favorites." There was the interview from Wednesday where I said Mrs. Fleck "pushes her kids too hard," which made some people in the front yard hoot with approval. And it showed a short interview with Nana, where she said, "I've never been more proud of him in my entire life. Plus, we play cards all day long, it's wonderful!"

Mrs. Fleck wasn't on there, though. I guess they were saving her for the live show.

After the video ended, the lights came up and Brody announced, "Back to talk with Jack Strong, after these short messages."

During the commercial break, the makeup people came out and attacked Brody's face, while barely touching mine. "You're younger than me, you don't need as much help," he said.

The stage lights came back on.

"Welcome back to *Kidz in the Newz*. And now, at last, Jack Strong." The applause signs flashed, and Brody turned to me.

"Jack, tell us how the whole thing began."

After all the waiting, and all the sitting, and all the sweating, I was ready.

I took a deep breath.

"Well, like you said, one day after school, I was sitting on the couch, and my mom came to get me for soccer practice, and I told her I didn't want to go."

Brody looked at me, waiting. "And . . . ?"

I wasn't sure what else to say. He'd basically just told everyone the story. But Brody kept looking at me, so I told it again. "And . . . I told my parents I wanted to quit some of the activities that they made me do. And they didn't let me. They said I needed to be well rounded to get into college. So I decided to go on strike and stay on the couch until they changed their minds."

"Let's talk about your dad," Brody said. "This is mainly his doing, correct? This obsession with getting into a good college?"

"I guess."

"So how has he reacted to this whole thing? Why do you think he hasn't just let you have your way? Are you disappointed he's not here tonight to tell us his side of the story? What's his deal?"

I wasn't expecting those questions.

"I thought we were going to talk about the problem of kids being overscheduled," I finally stammered. "I don't really want to talk about my dad."

"But your dad is part of the problem, right?"

I froze, suddenly wishing I hadn't gone on strike at all.

"This is obviously a complicated issue, on both sides," Brody continued, after realizing that I wasn't going to say anything bad about my dad. "And speaking of both sides, I'd like to bring up a woman who is the leading voice from the parents' point of view. Ladies and gentlemen, Missy Fleck."

The crowd applauded politely, with some scattered booing, as Mrs. Fleck made her way to the stage.

When she got up to the stage, the first thing she did was hold out her hand to me. I shook it.

"Nice to see you, Jack," she said.

"You, too," I answered.

"Please, sit down," Brody said.

"Where?" she asked. Brody pointed to the couch. My couch! She looked at me, and I shrugged.

"Plenty of room," I said, and the audience giggled nervously.

Mrs. Fleck sat down on the couch.

"Mrs. Fleck," Brody began, "you are on record as saying that Jack is setting a dangerous example to kids everywhere. Can you explain?"

"I sure can," she said. "But first, let me say that I think Jack is a fine boy, and I'm sure he'll be very successful in whatever he does." Then she flashed the same look that made me drop my bow in the cello recital. "In fact, my guess is that, ironically, this whole episode will help him a great deal when it comes time for him to apply to college. For all I know, that's part of the plan!"

I couldn't believe this woman. Mrs. Fleck hated what I was doing and was jealous of me, all at the same time!

"But here's my problem," she continued. "It's a tough world out there, and getting tougher every day. Children today don't realize how hard it is to make it. They think they can just coast along until one day a good job will just be handed to them on a silver platter. Well, it doesn't work that way. It takes hard work, very hard work. And the sooner we teach the value of hard work to our children, the better off they'll be in the long run."

"Very interesting perspective, Mrs. Fleck," Brody said. Then he looked at me. "And one I suspect your father agrees with, right Jack?"

I looked straight at Mrs. Fleck. "Actually, even my

dad thinks you're kind of over the top," I answered to laughter and applause.

Brody laughed, too, then nodded to someone off-stage. "So there you have it, both sides of the story," he said, "and two compelling arguments. But now, I want to bring out our surprise guest. She has a unique perspective on our discussion tonight, and I'm sure we all want to hear what she has to say."

He pointed to a dark corner of the stage. "Ladies and gentlemen, please welcome Lucy Fleck."

Everyone turned as Lucy emerged out of the shadows.

Oh great, I thought. So that's why she'd been calling me. To tell me she was going to make me look bad on live TV.

I quickly turned to look at Mrs. Fleck, who was smiling at her daughter.

Her daughter didn't smile back.

Lucy nervously walked over and sat down next to me on the couch. We glanced at each other. The audience was dead silent.

"Hey," she said.

"Hey," I said back.

"So, Lucy," Brody began, "you are the daughter of Missy Fleck, whose opinion we've just heard. I'm sure we're all very curious to hear where you stand on this whole thing. Do you share your mom's views? Is Jack doing the wrong thing?"

Lucy looked around, her eyes getting wider and wider, and she seemed really nervous. For a minute, I wasn't sure she'd be able to say anything at all.

But as it turned out, she was braver than me.

"Actually, I agree with Jack," she said, in a voice so soft only Brody, Mrs. Fleck, and I could hear her.

Mrs. Fleck's eyes started popping out of her head.

"Can you say that again?" Brody asked gently.

"I agree with Jack," Lucy repeated a little louder. "I think he's doing a good thing. I know my mom has my best interests at heart, but sometimes it's too much. It makes me scared and sad and sometimes angry and stuff like that. And it's not fun."

By now her voice was at full strength. Lucy looked straight at her mother.

"I love you, Mom, but sometimes I just want to be a kid."

Mrs. Fleck stared at her daughter. "Lucy . . ." she said, but she couldn't finish the sentence.

"I know you love me," Lucy continued. "Please don't be mad."

Then she hugged her mom.

"Sorry," Lucy whispered.

Mrs. Fleck didn't say anything. But she did hug her daughter back.

Watching them, I suddenly missed my dad a lot.

"Wow, a powerful moment between mother and daughter," Brody said. "And now we want to hear from you, our audience. Where do you stand? Is Jack a brave pioneer or a lazy kid?"

He gave a thumbs-up motion to somebody, the lights came up on the audience, and a young guy in a suit started running around with a microphone in his hand.

The first person to speak was some high school kid I didn't recognize. "These parents are lunatics! I support the kids!"

An older woman spoke next. "You're wrong! Kids today are lazy! Jack's the laziest of them all!"

Then some guy didn't even wait for the mike, he just started pointing at me and yelling. "Why is this young man so determined to hurt his parents?"

And that was it. All of a sudden, it was a free-for-all.

"Let kids be kids!"

"Spoiled brats are what's wrong with this country!"

"I think he's a hero!"

"What's next, are kids going to refuse to do homework? Give me a break!"

Then Ricky, the guy who worked in the ice cream store decided to chime in. He'd defend me, right?

Wrong.

"You're a great kid, Jack, but you're a little spoiled," he said. "I wouldn't mind having had some of the opportunities you have. My parents couldn't have paid for Chinese lessons, that's for sure. I can't even afford to go to college this semester." Ricky nodded at me apologetically. "Sorry, kid, just calling it the way I see it," he added as half the audience clapped and half booed.

Meanwhile, I suddenly felt like the biggest jerk in the world.

Finally a familiar face came to my rescue. "I think what Jack is doing is AWESOME!" Baxter Billows yelled, and other kids roared. "Why should we have to run around worrying about college? We're kids! Let us be kids!"

But then someone else grabbed the mike. It was

Alex Mutchnik, the annoying kid from school whose favorite activity was knocking over my backpack. "I disagree with Baxter," he said. "I think Jack's just lazy. While we've been in school working hard, he's been home playing cards with his grandma."

That led to everyone arguing with each other all over again. I couldn't believe it. What I thought was going to be a show about me taking a stand was turning into a circus. I looked at Brody for help, but he was smiling and pretending to look at his index cards. I realized this was what he'd wanted all along. Good television.

I couldn't believe it. And as I listened to the craziness, one thing became clear.

No one actually cared what I thought.

I searched the crowd for my family. I saw my mom, yelling at some technician, trying to get him to pull the plug. I saw Nana, who was busy arguing with the guy who had said I was determined to hurt my parents.

But no sign of my dad.

People started screaming louder. Some lady in the front row yelped, "Success is hard work!" while someone else in the back row cried, "Life isn't easy! Kids need to be prepared!" Meanwhile, Cathy, Baxter, Leo, and Kevin Kessler were chanting, "Take a stand by taking a seat! Take a stand by taking a seat!" The string quartet at Mrs. Fleck's block party started playing "Workin' Day and Night" by Michael Jackson. Everyone was yelling, and nobody was listening to a word anyone else was saying.

Finally one voice rose above the rest.

"Can we have some quiet please? QUIET PLEASE!"

Nana.

Everyone stopped and turned to look at her. She was shaking a little bit, probably because she was about as mad as I've ever seen her in my life.

"That's enough!" said Nana. "Can you people hear yourselves? Have we all gone crazy? Can we all take a step back and remember whom this is about? The kids. It's about the kids."

Nana walked to the stage, where Larry helped her up the stairs. First she cornered Brody.

"I know what you're after." She told him. "You're after good television. Well, you got it. But at what expense? At the expense of my grandson, who's become nothing more than an animal in the zoo?" She looked out into the crowd and across the street. "And what about Mrs. Fleck and her supporters? You can agree or disagree with their methods, but they, too, are just trying to do the right thing for the children." Then Nana went over and put her hand gently on Lucy's cheek. "And this adorable girl, who is so brave—why are we making her discuss such personal, painful issues in such a public way?"

Nana turned out to the audience. "Shame on us. Shame on all of us for letting it get to this point. We need to trust our kids, just the way *we* wanted to be trusted when we were kids. We need to let them show us the way. Not the other way around."

Finally, she came over to me. "Jack is showing me the way. And I think it's wonderful."

Nana kissed my cheek as people cheered wildly. She smiled as she walked into the crowd to shake some peoples' hands, but I noticed she looked older than usual. Her skin was clammy, and her eyes were glassy. I saw her wince in pain, and it looked like she was having trouble breathing. At first I thought that she was just tired from her speech, but then I realized it was more than that.

Something was wrong.

I looked at my mom, who was thinking the same thing. She was trying to get to her mom, but was blocked by the crowd.

So I jumped off the couch and ran to Nana.

People couldn't believe it. "Hey, look! The strike's over! Jack Strong is off the couch! He's giving up!" Some people started cheering, some started booing. My friends started screaming at me to sit down again. No one understood what was happening. People were hugging me and grabbing me and pointing and laughing at me, but I didn't care. I just wanted to get them off me so I could get to my grandmother, but there were too many people.

Then, for some reason, I turned and looked down the street.

There was my dad, running up the block.

He'd made it after all.

He had a shocked expression on his face, and he started sprinting faster and faster. When he finally reached me, he yelled as loud as I've ever heard him yell.

"HANDS OFF MY SON!"

As people backed off, he pulled me out of the crowd and gave me a quick, strong hug. Then we ran to Nana, who was about to sit down.

My mom, my dad, and I reached her at the exact same time. We all hugged each other for a long moment and asked Nana if she was okay.

She smiled, and said, "Yes, of course! The family is together again."

Then she fell to the ground and collapsed.

38

It felt like time stopped. I wasn't sure if she was breathing or not. But somehow I knew exactly what to do.

I pressed down on her chest, and then I tilted her head back and blew into her mouth.

It didn't taste like wet socks.

Now, I'd like to tell you that this is where I saved Nana's life by giving her CPR for ten minutes, and by keeping her breathing until the ambulance got there. But the truth is, after about two seconds I felt a huge hand on my shoulder.

"Let me," Larry the Beard said.

I stood up as Larry bent down and pressed down on Nana's chest hard and quick, a bunch of times. Then he gave her two quick mouth-to-mouth breaths. Then he repeated the process, and repeated it again. Finally her chest gave a big heave.

Larry looked up.

"She's breathing," he said.

My mother started crying. My dad held her. A doctor who had been in the audience took care of Nana while someone called 911.

As we waited for the ambulance, Larry came over to me.

"You did good," he said.

"Thanks. So did you."

"Yeah, well, that's show biz." He stroked his big beard. "Did you take a course in CPR?"

I nodded. "Yeah."

Larry nodded back.

"That's one activity that might be worth getting off the couch for," he said.

39

Hospitals kind of freak me out.

The walls are really white. The floors are really shiny. The whole place has that gross overly clean smell. And everyone is whispering.

My goal in life is to hang out in hospitals as little as possible.

Luckily, Nana's nurse, who was named Jagadesh, was a really friendly person.

Plus, he recognized me.

"You're Jack Strong," he said, as we waited for the doctor to bring us some news.

"Yes," I answered, a little out of breath. Walking up the stairs from the underground parking lot to the lobby was the most non-yoga exercise I'd had in almost two weeks.

"I admire what you're doing," said Jagadesh. "Standing up for your rights. Very cool."

I tried to smile, but I was too worried. Nana

didn't look good at all when they took her out of the ambulance and into the emergency room. She tried to wave at me but her mouth was covered by an oxygen mask and she had tubes running to her arms.

When I saw her go through the hospital doors I'd started to cry a little bit, but I didn't want my parents to see me so I made myself stop. My mom was already very scared, and if she saw me crying that definitely would have made it worse.

In the waiting room, my parents sat down. My dad looked at me and pointed to a couch.

"No, thanks," I said. "I'd rather stand."

We all laughed at that and felt a little bit better.

And then we waited.

There was a television in the waiting room, and it was tuned to Brody's show. It was just ending, since it had taken us about fifteen minutes to get to the hospital and fifteen more to fill out the paperwork.

Brody and Shaina were talking at the desk on the stage, in our front yard. Watching them almost didn't feel real.

"This has been a memorable night, for so many reasons," Brody said.

"I've never seen anything like it," Shaina agreed.

"I sure hope that wonderful woman is okay," Brody added.

My dad got up and turned off the TV.

When he got back to the couch, he hugged my mom for a long time.

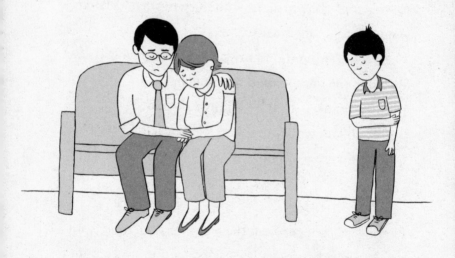

About an hour later the doctor came out. She looked young enough to be my sister, but my parents looked at her like she had the fate of the world in her hands. Which, in a way, she did.

"I'm Dr. Worsfold," she said, shaking my parents' hands. "You must be Mrs. Kellerman's daughter."

My mom stepped forward and nodded.

"Your mother went into cardiac arrest," said the doctor. "We're still working to restore a normal heart rate. We should know more in the next hour or so."

My mom managed to nod. "Thank you, Doctor."

"She's a real fighter," said Dr. Worsfold.

My mom nodded again and started to cry. My dad hugged her, then turned to the doctor.

"Tell me about it," he said.

40

After another hour or so, Dr. Worsfold came back to tell us that Nana had stabilized, but that she needed emergency angioplasty.

"It's a common procedure," the doctor explained, "but at Rose's age, of course, any surgery is a risk."

My parents looked at each other.

"I think she'll be just fine, but unfortunately there are no guarantees," the doctor added, answering the unasked question.

"Of course," said my mom. "Well, let's get to it then. The sooner the better."

With my parents' permission, Jagadesh arranged it so I could be the last one to talk to Nana before she went into the operating room.

A bunch of doctors and nurses and technicians were hurrying in and out of Nana's room, checking instruments, writing in charts, and examining every inch of her body. She saw me come in and rolled her eyes.

"I haven't had this many people fawn over me since before I was married," she said. Then she patted the bed. "Come sit."

I wasn't sure what to say. "Good luck" sounded kind of dumb and "I hope everything goes okay" sounded negative.

So I just said, "I love you, Nana."

She hugged me as hard as she could, which wasn't very hard. "I love you, too, Moochie-Pooch." Then she pushed me back so she could look at me. "This has been quite a couple of weeks, hasn't it?"

"Yup."

She hoisted herself up on her pillows. "I meant every word I said. I'm so proud of you. But now it's time to get back to living."

"I know," I said, looking at the shiny white floor.

"Life is short, Jack," said Nana. "Too short to be doing things you don't want to do. But way too short to not be doing anything at all."

I nodded, and she lay back down on the bed, tired from the effort of talking. The doctors told us it was time to go. As she was getting wheeled away, Nana looked up at me.

"Meet me back here in three hours for *Law & Order*."

41

Have you ever eaten hospital cafeteria food? It turns out it's pretty good. Especially the chocolate pudding.

During Nana's surgery, we all went to get something to eat. My dad and I both ate pudding. My mom had a sandwich, but she was staring at it more than eating it. No one said anything for a while.

Finally I looked up.

"Mom? Dad? I've decided to end my strike."

"That's wonderful news, honey!" my mom exclaimed.

My dad kept working on his pudding. He'd barely said a word since we got to the hospital, and I couldn't tell what he was thinking.

"Starting tomorrow," I went on. "There's the first baseball summer league tryout, and I want to go. And I want to go to orchestra rehearsal, too. I want to concentrate on baseball and cello. Those are the things I love and those are the things I want to do. And I know how lucky I am that I get to do them."

I waited, thinking my dad would say something, but he didn't.

"And there are a lot of other things I might want to do that I don't even know about yet. Like work in a kitchen supply store, for example."

My dad still didn't look up, but I think I saw him smile just a little bit at the reference to his childhood.

"And Junior EMTs," said my mother.

"And Junior EMTs," I agreed.

"But I shouldn't have to do all that stuff I don't want to do," I went on. "Life's too short for that, just like Nana says." I stopped, trying not to cry. "And how can you argue with a woman whose heart is working overtime?"

Mom smiled. I had one last thing to say.

"Plus, I think we can all agree that this is going to look pretty awesome on my college application."

My dad finally looked up.

"Now you're talking my language," he said.

I laughed, because I wasn't sure what else to do. Then I waited. My dad put down his spoon, picked up his tray, and threw out his garbage. Then he refilled his coffee cup and got back on line for some more food. I think he was stalling. Finally, he came back over and sat down.

"The day I left for college, it was raining," he said. "The drive should have taken three hours, but it took five. My mom drove the whole way, with my dad doing the navigating. I sat in the back." He took a sip of coffee. "I think we said maybe ten words to each other the whole way up."

"How come?" I asked.

He shook his head. "It was the biggest day of my life, but it was almost too big. Nobody could think of anything to say."

I sat, waiting, knowing he wasn't done.

"Finally we got there, my mom makes my bed, my dad puts a few posters on the wall. Then, it was time for them to get going. None of us wanted a long drawn-out thing, though. So I hugged my mom, and we said our I-love-yous and goodbyes. Then I hugged my dad, but not too hard, because he'd already lost a lot of weight by then. He was still quiet, but I couldn't let him go without saying something. So I said, 'I'll make you proud, dad, I promise.'"

My father looked up at the hospital ceiling—maybe

through the ceiling, actually, up to the sky and beyond, maybe to his own father.

"Dad just looked at me," he said. "Then he shook his head once and said, 'You already have, son. You already have.'"

My dad stopped for a second. My mom took his hand and squeezed it.

Then he turned and looked straight at me.

"I don't want to say I'm wrong and you're right," he said. "That might be the case, but I'm not ready to say that just yet." He put his hand on my shoulder. "But you know how I always talk about how finding

your 'thing' is so important?" I nodded. Did I ever! That's how this whole craziness started.

"Well, maybe you've already found it," my dad said. "Because sticking up for what you believe in is the greatest thing of all."

My heart felt huge in my chest, and I wasn't sure I could talk. But I managed to say two words. "Thanks, Dad."

He let out a big, exhausted sigh. "So now, back to the matter at hand. I tried to make it back to the TV show to say this on the air, but your nana beat me to it. You shouldn't have to do things you have absolutely no interest in. I can't argue with that." He looked at my mom, then back at me. "But the things you are inter-ested in, I want you to pursue with all your heart." He held out his hand. "Fair enough?"

We shook. "Fair enough."

My dad hugged me, and I hugged him back. Then he pointed at his tray, and I noticed he'd just bought two more chocolate puddings.

"You can't have enough pudding," he said, giving me one.

I dug in. It was the best pudding I'd ever eaten.

A few minutes later the door to the cafeteria opened,

and we saw Dr. Worsfold coming toward us with a serious expression on her face. My parents stood up. I felt a nervous jolt.

"Mrs. Strong," the doctor said.

My mom took my father's hand. "Yes?"

Dr. Worsfold smiled, and the world relaxed.

"Your mother is asking for a tongue sandwich."

42

Nana was going to be sleeping most of the night, so my parents decided it was time to take me home so I could get some sleep.

When we stepped into the hospital lobby, I saw about five cameras, ten reporters, and twenty people. I wondered who they were waiting for, and then realized they were waiting for me.

I saw Lucy Fleck and her mother. I saw Leo, Cathy, and Baxter Billows.

Cathy came running up and gave me a kiss on the cheek. "You're awesome," she whispered.

I'll take "awesome" over "kind of funny" any day.

I saw Larry, the huge bearded guy who'd helped Nana when she collapsed. He waved.

The reporters ran toward me. Shaina Townsend reached me first.

"How's your grandmother?"

I gave a thumbs-up. "She's going to be okay," I said, and everyone cheered.

"And what about you, Jack?" asked Shaina. "Are you going to be okay? What about the strike? What's your plan?"

I looked straight into the cameras. "I've decided to end the strike. My family and I worked it all out. I can't wait to get back to school and my friends and doing the things I love."

The crowd started chanting something, but I couldn't tell what they were saying at first. Then I could.

They were chanting, "Jack! Jack! Jack!"

I gave another thumbs-up and started walking toward the car, but Shaina stopped me.

"Someone wants to say something to you," Shaina said. I saw Mrs. Fleck emerge from the crowd. Lucy was next to her, and she had some flowers in her hand.

Mrs. Fleck nodded at her daughter, and Lucy gave them to me.

"These are for your grandmother," Lucy said.

I leaned into them and inhaled. They smelled amazing. "Thank you, Mrs. Fleck. Thank you, Lucy."

"Thank *you*," Lucy said to me.

Mrs. Fleck handed me a gift. I opened it—it was a

CD of music by Pablo Casals, the amazing cellist who had almost certainly never dropped his bow.

"I look forward to hearing you play again," Mrs. Fleck said.

I shook her hand. "Me, too," I said. "Me, too."

I hugged Lucy. Then I shook hands with Larry, high-fived Leo, accepted another kiss on the cheek from Cathy and a punch on the arm from Baxter, and waved to everyone else. Then I got in my parents' car and drove back to our house.

And back to real life.

EPILOGUE

JACK'S SCHEDULE

DATE	20	21	22
DAY	MONDAY	TUESDAY	WEDNESDAY
TIME	7:30 SCHOOL	7:30 SCHOOL	7:30 SCHOOL
TIME	6:00 DINNER	5:30 LITTLE LEAGUE ALL-STAR GAME	7:30 DINNER
TIME	7:00 HOMEWORK	7:30 DINNER	9:30 CELLO PRACTICE
TIME	8:30 CELLO PRACTICE	8:30 HOMEWORK	10:00 BED
TIME	9:30 BED	9:30 BED	
TIME			

23 THURSDAY	24 FRIDAY	25 SATURDAY	SUNDAY
7:30 SCHOOL	7:30 SCHOOL	9:00 YOUTH ORCHESTRA	10:00 CELLO LESSON
6:00 DINNER	6:45 DINNER	7:00 DINNER	12:00 JUNIOR EMTs
9:00 CELLO PRACTICE	7:30 MOVIE NIGHT	10:00 BED	7:00 DINNER
9:45 BED	10:00 BED		9:30 BED

So that's my story.

I still go to Horace Henchell Middle School, and Horace is still dead. The hallways are still a grimy yellow, the classrooms are still way too hot, and the cheeseburgers are still way too cold. And Alex Mutchnik is still in my class.

But it's okay. I don't mind Horace so much, or his school. In fact, I like it a lot more now. It's fun, and it's hard but not that hard, and it's just a normal part of my normal life.

I still play the cello, which I'm really good at; and I still play baseball, which I'm not that good at. But no more tennis or karate or swimming or tutors. I have some free time now, which I mostly spend hanging out with friends, reading, playing video games, and wrestling with my dog.

Nana and I do yoga together every day.

My dad is good with all the changes and everything, but he still talks about China, and how important it is. He asks me about once a week if I would consider giving Chinese another try. I told him that maybe I'd consider taking it in high school.

We'll just have to wait and see on that one.

When Nana came home from the hospital, she looked tired but healthy. She was pretty grumpy, though, because Dr. Worsfold told her that tongue sandwiches were off-limits: way too salty for her strict new diet.

The first night she was home, she was having trouble falling asleep, so she asked me to play the cello for her. I played for thirty-five minutes straight, concentrating on nothing but the music. It felt so good.

When I finally stopped to ask Nana if she wanted me to play more, she was snoring so loudly I thought the walls might cave in.

On Monday, my first day back at school, which also happened to be the start of the last week of the school year, Cathy Billows, who's still so pretty that it makes my eyebrows hurt, came running up to me.

"Jack's back! Yay!!! Hey, everyone, Jack's here!" Exclamation points were flying all over the place.

All day, I was treated like a king. At lunch, Mrs. Bondetto, the head cafeteria lady, gave me an extra chocolate chip cookie AND an extra chocolate milk. In English class, Mrs. Bender gave me a big hug, with her tiny but unmistakable mustache brushing my cheek. Mr. Lahiff, the gym teacher, let me skip the annoying pommel horse. And at recess, all the kids wanted me on their basketball team, but I decided to just hang out on the sideline with Leo and Lucy.

Then, at the end of the day, Cathy pulled me aside.

"The End-of-Year Dance is coming up on Friday!"

"Cool."

"So, do you think you would want to go with me?"

This was it. The moment I'd been waiting for from the first moment I realized girls existed, about halfway through third grade. Cathy Billows was inviting me to a dance.

I shook my head.

"I can't," I said. "I forgot all about the dance, so I made other plans for Friday night."

Cathy's face went a little dark, the way it did when I told her I couldn't go to her party two weeks earlier. But this time, she snapped right out of it and gave me a bright smile.

"What kind of plans?"

"You wouldn't be interested, I don't think."

"Try me!"

So I told her.

The next day, Tuesday, was the Little League All-Star game. Even though I wasn't exactly an all-star, the coaches decided to let me play. Maybe they thought Brody Newhouse would come and cover it, but he didn't. In any case, I was batting against Kevin Kessler, the strikeout king. It was the bottom of the sixth (and last) inning, with us losing by one, one out and a man on third.

My dad was in the stands, videotaping. My mom was yakking to another mother. And Maddie was grazing on dropped French fries.

Just like always.

The count quickly went to no balls and two strikes. Kevin wound up and fired. I took a mighty swing . . . and fouled it off.

Contact! That felt good.

Then Kevin threw me three straight balls. I stepped out of the batter's box, thinking about how this was just like the last time I was up, in the World Series. I'd worked the count full from 0–2, then hit the epic pop-up to second base that won the championship.

Holy moly! Would I be the hero again?

Kevin checked the runner at third, stared in at me, then reared back and let fly. The pitch came. It looked outside. A walk! Awesome! I could go to first and let Kevin Kessler be someone else's problem. I was totally good with that.

Only, the pitch wasn't outside. It was on the outside corner. I watched it go by with a sinking feeling.

"Strike three!" yelled the umpire, who happened to be Alex Mutchnik's older brother, Henry. I think he was smiling when he said it.

I trudged back to the dugout and threw my helmet.

"Easy there, Jack," said the coach, Mr. Bonner, whose main claim to fame was that he could spit sunflower seeds farther than any human being alive.

"Sorry, coach," I said.

I sat down on the bench. Other kids came over and said things to try and make me feel better. It was pretty clear I wasn't a big deal anymore. I was just another kid who struck out. But as I looked around and watched everybody root for Ben Liscomb, who was up next, I realized something.

It felt great.

Then it was Friday. I got on the bus to go home, sitting in my usual seat: third row, window seat on the left. But one thing was different: the seat next to me was never empty anymore, because people always seemed to want to sit next to me.

That day, Alex Mutchnik decided to plop down.

I immediately grabbed my backpack before he could do anything to it, but it turned out he wasn't interested in that.

"Can I ask you a question?" he said.

"I guess."

He looked around the bus. "So, my parents are telling me that I have to do like some community service thing this summer, and maybe like take a class or something. I really don't feel like doing any of that stuff. I just want to hang out and chill, you know? Like, the way you do. What should I tell them? Or better yet, do you think you could talk to them?"

I had to laugh. Alex Mutchnik, asking me for help!

"Listen Alex, I'd love to help you out, but maybe doing a little volunteer work this summer is a good idea. I do EMT training, you know."

"You do? I thought you hated all that stuff."

I rolled my eyes. "I don't hate all that stuff. I just want to do things I want to do, that's all. Volunteer work is cool as long as you do it, and not your parents."

Alex looked at me, then decided he was done being

nice to me. "Whatever," he mumbled. Then he grabbed my backpack out of my hands and threw it onto the floor.

Just like old times.

The school bus headed for home, and it couldn't get there fast enough. That night, Leo and Lucy were coming over for a marathon of Bruce Lee's classic Hong Kong martial arts movies. Not only that, but after I'd told Cathy that our movie marathon was the reason I couldn't go to the school dance, she'd decided to come too, and bring her brother Baxter. My dad was going to grill some burgers and dogs, my mom was going to make a salad that no one would eat, and Nana was going to make some of her legendary chocolate chip cookies.

"Why Bruce Lee movies?" Cathy asked, when I told her the plan.

"It was my dad's idea. He thought I should get some use out of my Chinese-English dictionary before we gave it away," I said.

Cathy thought about that for a second. "That makes perfect sense," she said.

Using my jacket as a pillow just like always, I rested my head against the bus window and smiled, thinking about the night ahead. It was going to be completely perfect, because it combined all of my favorite things: cheeseburgers, movies, family, friends, and dessert.

And the couch.

In memory of Ellen Kellerman
1913–2012

"You bettah do."

ACKNOWLEDGMENTS

I would like the following people to sit down and take a bow:

Everyone at Macmillan/Roaring Brook, who continue to amaze me.

Nancy Conescu, an early friend of Jack Strong's.

Lauren Tarshis, who suggested I make Jack a friend of Charlie Joe's.

Gina Green, who helps me deal with my own over-scheduled schedule and keeps me sane in the process.

Brianne Johnson, who is always helpful and always cheerful.

Susan Cohen, for jumping into the fray.

Barbara Kellerman and Jonathan Greenwald, who never made me do anything I didn't want to do. (Well, almost never.)

And Cathy Utz, who has sat next to me on the couch every night for twenty-five years.

Go Fish!

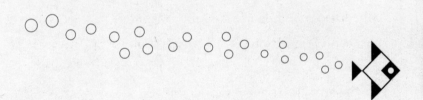

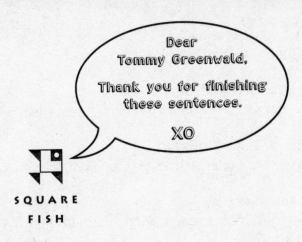

Sometimes I wish . . .
french fries were good for you.

When I was a kid . . .
I didn't play video games. Because they WEREN'T INVENTED YET. (Yup, I'm old.)

Chinese lessons are . . .
very helpful when ordering Chinese food.

My schedule is . . .
a little crazy, but crazy with stuff I love.

Jack Strong should . . .
never use his cello as a baseball bat.

My couch . . .
is one of my favorite places in the whole wide world.

Tongue sandwiches are . . .
  probably illegal in several states.

Cello practice and Junior EMTs . . .
  are not often used in the same sentence.

Charlie Joe Jackson is . . .
  less of a loudmouth in this book than he usually is.

Katie Friedman likes . . .
  the fact that she's now the star of her OWN book.

Telling stories . . .
  is the most fun job a guy could ever have. Except for ice cream taster.

I've never . . .
  eaten a tomato.

Authors often . . .
  spend too much time doing anything other than writing.

But why didn't you ask me about . . .
  my dogs? I LOVE talking about my dogs!

WHEN A TEXT MESSAGE GOES WRONG,
KATIE FRIEDMAN LEARNS THE HARD WAY THAT
SOMETIMES YOU NEED TO DISCONNECT TO CONNECT.

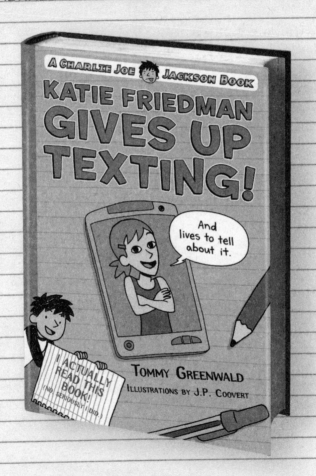

KEEP READING TO FIND OUT IF KATIE CAN
REALLY GIVE UP TEXTING . . .

INTRODUCTIONS

Hey, everyone—nice to see you. It's me, Katie Friedman.

You guys remember me, right?

I'm the one who's usually cheering on the sidelines while Charlie Joe Jackson tells you all those heroic stories about how awesome he is. But he's not all that awesome. He's lazy, conceited, and obnoxious. He's also been my best friend since kindergarten.

♥ ♥ ♥

But enough about him.

Let's talk about me.

♥ ♥ ♥

I have an important question to ask you.

Are you doing something else besides reading this book right now?

Are you texting, or Instagraming, or watching a TV show online, or anything like that?

Are you FaceTiming with anyone?

Are you checking Facebook? Snapchat? Twitter?

Are you on Face-Twit-Chat-Gram?

I know, Face-Twit-Chat-Gram doesn't exist.

Yet.

But it might by the time I finish writing this book.

Or you finish reading it.

Can I ask you something else?

Are you ever worried that screens might run your life?

And maybe ruin your life, too?

I didn't think so.

I wasn't worried, either.

I should have been.

Part 1
JANE'S DEAL

A BUSY MORNING

Here's what happened *before* breakfast on Monday, April 23:

I texted Hannah Spivero: `I need to talk to you at lunch.`

She texted me back: `About what?`

I texted her back: `Stuff`

She texted me back: `What kind of stuff?`

I texted her back: `Nareem stuff.`

She texted me back. `Got it. KK`

♥ ♥ ♥

I posted a picture of my dog staring at herself in the mirror.

♥ ♥ ♥

I got a text from Becca Clausen: `Mom says yes to rehearsal wednesday`

I texted her back: `Yay! Lots to do! Talent show in two weeks! Should we rehearse Saturday, too?`

She texted me back: `Dunno, might have basketball`

I texted her back: `Noooooooo`

♥ ♥ ♥

Then I texted Charlie Joe Jackson: `Ugh`

He texted me back: `What?`

I texted him back: `Nareem thing`

He texted me back: `Oooh`

♥ ♥ ♥

Then I got in the shower.

♥ ♥ ♥

Here's what happened *during* breakfast on Monday, April 23:

I got a text from Nareem Ramdal: `Hey`

I texted him back: `Hey`

He texted me back: `See you at school`

I texted him back: `Yup`

♥ ♥ ♥

Then I got a text from Eliza Collins: `Hi Katie!`

I texted her back: `Hi`

She texted me back: `Did you do the math?`

I texted her back: `Yes`

She texted me back: `Can i take a quick look in homeroom?`

I texted her back: `Again?`

She texted me back: `Last time i swear!!!`

I texted her back: `I guess`

She texted me back: `You're the best!`

♥ ♥ ♥

I texted Hannah: `Eliza is driving me crazy`

Hannah texted me back: `Duh`

I texted Hannah back: `Can't take it anymore.`

♥ ♥ ♥

Then I texted Becca: `Can Sammie bring her drums to rehearsal?`

I got a text back: `Dunno will ask her`

Then I looked up and saw my parents looking at me. They were both shaking their heads.

♥ ♥ ♥

Here's what happened *on the bus ride to school* on Monday, April 23:

I texted Charlie Joe: `Eliza is so annoying sometimes`

I got a text from Charlie Joe: `Sometimes?`

♥ ♥ ♥

Then I texted my mom: `Are you picking me up after school?`

She texted me back: `Can't, working, take bus okay?`

I texted her back: `K`

She texted me back: `K is not a word, and stop texting in school.`

I texted her back: `I'm on the bus`

She texted me back: `Got to go, love you honey.`

I texted her back: `K`

She texted me back: `Very funny.`

♥ ♥ ♥

I got another text from Charlie Joe: `Good luck with the Nareem thing`

I texted him back: `THX gonna need it`

♥ ♥ ♥

Then we got to school, and the day began.

All Charlie Joe.
All the time.

THE CHARLIE JOE JACKSON SERIES

Charlie Joe Jackson's
Guide to Not Reading
ISBN: 978-1-250-00337-9

Charlie Joe Jackson's
Guide to Extra Credit
ISBN: 978-1-250-01670-6

Charlie Joe Jackson's
Guide to Summer Vacation
ISBN: 978-1-62672-031-2

Charlie Joe Jackson's
Guide to Making Money
ISBN: 978-1-59643-840-8

COMING SOON!
Charlie Joe Jackson's
Guide to Planet Girl
ISBN: 978-1-59643-841-5